"AM Not"

"It's Time to Pray and Believe
Hell Is Risen!"

Mestat Imhotep

DEDICATION

For My Mother Who Always Believed in Me.

To my Late Fiancée, Tunisia R. Jones

And to the World in such times as these!

ACKNOWLEDGEMENTS

First and foremost, I would like to thank God, the Father, and Jesus, the Son. It was a vision given to me years ago, and the spirit in me decided to write a book about it so that the entire world can believe again.

I would like to thank my copy editor, Patricia Frazier at Frazier Enterprises, Inc., for helping me with my manuscript and being patient with me while working on this project.

To my beautiful, sweet mother (Sandra Butler): thank you for always believing in me and pushing me from the beginning of my writing journey to get it done by all means (Love you, Mom.)

To my late fiancée, Tunisia Regina Jones, her unconditional love and late nights, and her never-ending support while passing along a few ideas. (I finally did it; rest easy, Baby.)

To my little brother, Louis Butler, for the time we spent together talking about writing stories and getting them published someday.

To Regina Williams (my baby girl G), my number one fan for calling or texting me to never give up, and her special support towards my project.

Special thanks go to my friend—my sister from another mother—Violane McMillan Gillyard, who also encouraged me on this journey and her generous support also towards my project and her daughter, Sharon Jones, also my sister, for taking time out to make copies of my manuscript on her mother's copy machine. (I didn't own a copier at the time.)

To Kevin Fowler, my Late Fiancée's dad, thanks for accompanying me to my first writers' conference in downtown Philadelphia and reminding me to keep my head up and walk in with confidence.

Mr. K. from K's Moving, a friend and role model for getting things done.

To a dear, sweet friend whom I met on social media—Joyce Thurman— a business owner—at Escape the Ordinary. We didn't know each other at the time, when she called me to wish me nothing but love when I first started this project.

Her business is called Ms. Joyce's Travel Agency.

Other friends that I met on social media include Cassandra Valentine (Author); Anita Grace (Book Expert), Chistine Litworks (creator of stories that leave a lasting impact), Reds Garcia, Kelly Lawhorn, Rosemary Cartagena, Dana

Jamila Moss, Delois Sanders, and Henry Clyde Stromas, III.

Other family Members include:

Patricia Crawford, Tamika Cunningham McDougal, (Ernest Clinton—Politics as Usual); Angela Congleton, Kevin Banks, Davetta Smith, George Crawford, Eleanor Clinton, Susan Gadson, Diane Clinton, Crystal Lowery, Leonard Clinton, Shamika Clinton, Latisha Crawford Vasquez, Dawn Crawford, and many others. If you are in my circle, then you know much love from me is given to you as well!

Kimberly Smith—a big thanks to you for watching over my mother when I couldn't be present.

To my children, whom I love so dearly. A big thank-you from my heart goes to: Christopher, Cierra, Evangeline, Cardell, and Kanisha.

Finally, last but not least, a big, hearty thanks to Jake Thompson and Abby Keith, and the team members at McMillan Book writing.

God Bless!

CHAPTER 1

In the year of nineteen-sixty-nine, a raging storm appeared in Philadelphia with swirling winds and falling hail. It was a storm like never before. The moon reflected a dark red color and seemed larger than on any other night! Thousands of ravens flew in from the west in the dark gray skies and then suddenly vanished in midair. A two-headed rat crawled out from underneath a broken sewer pipe and began to nibble on the flesh of a stiff corpse that lay on a secluded parkway bench.

There were flash floods in most parts of the city. Interstate I-95 had closed down due to several accidents. Many drivers were taking the back roads to get to their destinations.

Sitting in the back seat of a local taxi that was departing from the Philadelphia International Airport were sixteen-year-old Alaysha and her mother, Catherine, who were arriving back from St. Peter's Square in Vatican City, a pilgrimage they undertook every November to receive a special blessing from the Pope!

The taxi driver began to slow down and focus his headlights on a homeless pedestrian crossing the street. She was slowly and repeatedly whispering: " The one that calls itself I AM is *coming and there shall be no peace!*"

Alaysha read the woman's lips from afar, and the old woman's words echoed in her ear, frightening her inner core. She desperately gripped her mother's arm and directed her attention toward the woman.

"Mom, did you hear that woman?"

"What did she say, Alaysha?" asked Catherine, looking baffled.

Catherine did not possess the same talent to read lips as her daughter; also, the woman was not close to them.

Before Alaysha could utter a word, the homeless woman walked over to the side door and peered through the back window as the driver stopped at the red light.

Suddenly, the wind pushed the woman against the window of the taxi's rear door, making a tremendous noise with a hard, banging sound that shook Catherine and her daughter into total fear. The woman then banged forcefully on the window.

"Damn the beast!"

The driver pressed his foot down on the gas pedal, crossed against the red light signal, and sped down the street, leaving a mist of black smoke.

"Crazy, psycho!" he yelled.

Alaysha and her mother, Catherine, had never experienced such a weird encounter in their lives!

The two held tightly onto one another. As they stared out the back window, from a distance, the strange, homeless woman mysteriously disappeared from their view in the midnight storm.

When they arrived home, a dreary sight appeared on the outside of their two-story house in Northeast Philadelphia, where they had lived since Catherine was an infant.

Apparently, lightning had struck a nearby tree that broke in half, falling inches from the taxi, followed by a loud, roaring, thunderous sound that shook the entire neighborhood.

Alaysha's grandmother, Ms. Florence, stood patiently at the front doorway with her arms crossed and a weary appearance on her face.

Catherine paid the driver for the ride and for carrying the luggage to the front door.

Distressed, scared, and tired, Alaysha ran past her grandmother into the house and up the stairs to her bedroom and slammed the door shut!

"What is wrong with that child?" asked Ms. Florence.

Catherine scratched her forehead. "We had a strange encounter tonight!"

"I did, too. I had a conversation with the Devil again," replied Ms. Florence with her left hand on her hip.

"It's time for you to see Mr. Silverman," said Catherine angrily, as she passed by her mother while heading to the kitchen.

Mr. Silverman was the psychiatrist who counseled Ms. Florence from time to time. After she had discovered her late husband's head in the oven burned to a crisp at a bakery they owned, she had changed in such a dramatic way. She began talking to herself and hearing voices. Later, Mr. Silverman diagnosed her as a schizophrenic.

When neither a suspect nor any hard evidence could be found, the Philadelphia authorities considered her husband's case as cold!

"I keep telling you, damn it, nothing is mentally wrong with me," yelled Ms. Florence as she followed behind Catherine.

Catherine turned around in a rage of fury. "So, what did you and the Devil talk about this time, Mama—going to hell?"

Ms. Florence stared for a second at Catherine in a sinister way. The words she'd spoken were hard to accept.

"Why do you talk as if Hell is a bad place? You know we're all going there someday!"

"Enough, Mama!" Catherine banged her hand on the kitchen counter. "You are the only one going to Hell in this house!"

Ms. Florence turned away quietly and went upstairs to her bedroom.

Catherine nodded her head and moved towards the wine cabinet for a drink to calm her nerves.

A knock at the front door alarmed Catherine for a moment. Then suddenly the door flew wide open with a gust of wind following. It was the old woman, the pedestrian whom she had encountered earlier.

"Damn the beast!" said the woman in a deep, heavy voice. She was naked and covered in blood. Catherine screamed; she ran over and slammed the front door.

Upon hearing the startling noise, Alaysha ran down the stairs. She immediately ran over and held her mother in her arms.

"What happened, Mom?" she asked, frightened.

"I don't know, honey!" They both were terrified. Ms. Florence came out of her room and stood at the top of the stairs with a peculiar smile on her face.

"The Devil told me this was going to happen," she laughed. "And you think I am the crazy one!" She turned away and went back into her room.

In a state of confusion, Catherine and Alaysha started upstairs to prepare for bed. A flash of light entered the front window. Where it came from was a mystery!

Writing on the wall

From the strange homeless woman

"You can't hide from evil;

It will find you every time!"

CHAPTER 2

The next day, Alaysha met up with Melissa, her best friend since kindergarten, in a secluded restaurant. They ordered their favorite meal—honey turkey with corned beef added on a Kaiser roll with coleslaw and a cold bottle of sweet tea for two. Alaysha was keenly aware that Melissa was anxious to hear about the trip and visiting the Pope for the hundredth time.

"So tell me about the Vatican," Melissa laughed as she bit into her sandwich.

"You ask the same question every year and get the same answer every time—very boring," Alaysha giggled, as she sipped on her bottle of sweet tea.

"It's not fair; you never tell me anything about your trip," Melissa mumbled after wiping the crumbs from her lip with a napkin.

Alaysha swirled her head and instead told her about the strange encounter she and her mother had had last night. After taking a swallow of tea, she gently slammed the bottle on the table, saying, "I have a secret to tell you!"

Melissa frowned, saying, "Don't tell me you're pregnant!"

"No, idiot, I met someone in Rome!" Before Alaysha could finish the conversation, she felt light-headed. A tremendously sharp pain rose in her stomach that caused her to let out a horrific moaning sound.

"What's the matter?" Melissa asked, looking deeply concerned.

Alaysha removed a napkin from the table and wiped the sweat off her forehead. "I don't feel right."

James, an older boy she had been secretly dating for a year and a half, entered the restaurant. When he kneeled down to kiss her on the cheek, he felt a weird vibe in the air. "What's wrong, Alaysha?"

Alaysha stood up quickly in an awkward position. As she reached out to smack James, she fell backwards, landed on the floor, and passed out.

Immediately, with Melissa's help, James lifted her up off the floor and placed her gently on one of the vacant tables. After he gave Alaysha mouth-to-mouth resuscitation, she immediately recovered, pushed him away, and ran out of the restaurant.

She arrived at her front porch, praying that no one was home. She heard voices coming from inside the house. She sat in silence, thinking of what to do next, until she felt a sudden tap on her shoulder that startled her. When she turned and looked up, James was standing there like a mental patient who had escaped from an institute. She stood up and punched him madly on his chest.

"What are you doing here?" She gripped hold of his hand and led him to the back of the house, where they sat quietly on the ground for a moment. The two then went quietly into the house through the basement window. After hearing their parents upstairs, they paused for a moment.

Catherine was talking about politics as usual with James' parents. Richard and Dorothy had been friends with Catherine since high school and happened to be neighbors.

James started to feel aroused; he forcefully took Alaysha in his arms and began kissing her with his wet tongue in her mouth.

She pushed him away suddenly when her stomach started to bulge a little. Startled, James's entire face turned red. He called out desperately for help and began to cough uncontrollably. He placed his hands tightly around his neck. Alaysha held her mouth; she wanted to scream. Just then, a black serpent crawled out of James' mouth, followed by an enormous amount of blood. He quickly stood up and ran up the stairs past his parents and out the front doorway.

"What the hell?" yelled Richard, as he ran behind James.

Catherine and Dorothy negotiated their way down into the basement.

Alaysha was stretched out in a puddle of blood with white foam oozing from her mouth. Catherine went ballistic!

Richard came running down the stairs with a terrified look on his face. He told his wife and Catherine that James had locked himself in the bathroom and threatened to kill himself. Catherine called the police. When the police finally arrived, she and Alaysha went to the hospital. When the police went next door to Richard and Dorothy's house, they found James dead on the bathroom floor with his throat slashed by his own hand.

Writing on the wall

From the strange homeless woman

Beware and watch at all times.

The one whose name is AM Not is coming!

CHAPTER 3

A man in his mid-fifties in the Middle East was commanded by a divine messenger to begin a search before the birth of the two infants and others that would follow. Some say he resembles Moses from the Bible. To many, he was granted the name Man of God. It had been three years since he had been sent on a mission searching for souls that were stamped from Hell!

There were certain people that had lived and passed away who were stamped before birth to perpetuate evil on Earth.

As he wiped his face with a warm cloth, a deep, unseen voice whispered, "Where will you begin, you so-called Man of God?"

"Let me be, Satan. Your days are numbered!" he whispered back to the unseen voice.

After packing his luggage, he headed for the exit. When he came out of his tent, two men escorted him to a nearby helicopter. Before he stepped foot on U.S. soil, a voice led him to visit the Pope.

Priest Thomas, the Pope's right-hand man, led him deep into the Vatican gardens. The Pope had been alone with a distressed appearance on his face.

"You sent for me, Papa?" he asked when Priest Thomas walked away.

The Pope removed a handkerchief from his side pocket and wiped the tears from his eyes.

"I have a heavy burden on my mind. These two Evil infants are about to be among us," said the Pope.

"A divine spirit told me," replied the Man of God.

"Find them and do it quickly," said the Pope.

The Man of God began his mission. He traveled to foreign countries to warn people about the coming of These two evil Infants from hell.

There were some that believed and others that did not believe in God or Satan!

"Pray, be mindful and watch," he said to the believers.

He began his search in New York City. While roaming the streets, he overheard a conversation about a nun leaving a convent and who committed the sinful act of getting pregnant. Filled with embarrassment, she hid herself around the convent property. A voice led him to the convent, where he met one of the sisters. When he explained the story he'd heard on the streets and also about the two evil infants, the nun overheard the conversation through a small open outside vent. When they searched for the nun, she could not be found.

Several hours later, her bloody body was discovered in the convent attic. She had stabbed herself in the stomach multiple times; she was scared to death it might have been herself that carried one of the Infants!

The search continued in Los Angeles, California. This time, the Man of God was led by a mysterious voice to homeless pregnant women on the streets that were also addicted to illegal drugs. A lot of them offered him sex for money. He gave money only to massage their stomachs to see if they carried the unwanted Infants. Still, it failed, although a few carried their followers.

These children, he knew, would grow up with damaged minds and mental depression. He started to feel that he needed to rest. He caught a taxi and asked the driver to take him to the nearest hotel. Suddenly, he realized the voice he had heard had been fraudulently placed in his mind. That night before going to sleep, an angel in a cloudy vision appeared before his eyes, saying, "Go now, Man of God, to a city that bears love or Washington, D.C. There, you will find the one that carries one of the Infants."

The next day, he took the first plane to Philadelphia, the "City of Brotherly Love".

Writing on the wall

From the strange homeless woman

He that practices in the left

Will never turn to the right.

CHAPTER 4

On the day of James' funeral, talk was escalating about his death among family members and close friends. Melissa looked around for Alaysha and noticed that she was not present. Little did she know that Alaysha had been hospitalized for a period of time. The last time the two had socialized was at their favorite restaurant the day Alaysha had run out. She visited her friend's house after James' burial.

When Melissa knocked on the front door, it opened slowly by itself. She crept her way in and up the stairs and then became startled by a strange sound and smell coming from Ms. Florence's room. She tiptoed quietly toward the half-opened door and peeped in. She became frantic when she saw Ms. Florence cutting off the tail of a dead black cat. She choked back a cough occasioned by the smell of the burning incense displayed in the corner of the room. She quickly covered her mouth and moved silently to the side wall and began walking down the hall toward Alaysha's room. A crackling sound disturbed her from behind. While turning around, to her surprise, Ms. Florence swung an axe, taking off Melissa's head.

"The Devil told me this was going to happen," yelled Ms. Florence.

"And you think I am the crazy one!"

Waiting for the test results, Catherine never left Alaysha's bedside during the entire time. The doctor calculated Alaysha's two-week pregnancy without sexual intercourse.

Bewildered and in a state of confusion, Catherine then left the hospital! When she drove up in a taxi near her house, Melissa's mother and a police officer were ringing the front doorbell.

"Can I help you?" she asked nervously as she walked up the steps.

"Have you seen Melissa?" asked the woman.

Catherine paused for a moment. "I have not seen Melissa in days!"

The police officer considerately handed Catherine a card with his name and number on it and told her if she heard anything to give him a call.

As Melissa's mother and the officer walked away, the front door opened unexpectedly. Before Catherine could go into the house, Ms. Florence stopped her and asked about Alaysha's condition.

"All this time I thought she was a virgin,!" said Catherine

Ms. Florence crossed her arms. "I thought the same thing when you were sixteen!"

"I'm not in the mood, Mama, not now!"

"The Devil . . ." Before Ms. Florence could finish her sentence, Catherine yelled out loud.

"Would you cut the Devil-told-me bull-shit, Mama!"

She pushed Ms. Florence to the side and charged into the house. She walked into the kitchen and reached into the cabinet for a bottle of red wine. Twisting the top off with her mouth, Catherine began drinking it straight down.

"Drinking is not going to take away what is happening," said Ms. Florence.

Catherine removed the bottle from her lips. "Mama, are you comprehending the words coming out of my mouth?"

"Yes, Catherine, the seed's been planted; you can't change what is meant to be!"

"What seed, Mama?"

"I cannot reveal that information."

Catherine slammed the bottle of red wine down on the kitchen table, causing it to shatter into pieces.

"You are so out of here, Mama. I am calling Mr. Silverman!"

Twenty-five minutes later, Mr. Silverman arrived. He was already in the area. Catherine left them alone and returned to the hospital.

Mr. Silverman sat down calmly on the living room couch and reached into his briefcase. He pulled out a tape recorder and set it on the table in front of him. Ms. Florence sat down on the other side of the couch. She watched him carefully as he pushed the button on the device to record their conversation.

"Have you been talking to Satan again, Ms. Florence?"

Ms. Florence smiled and crossed her legs. "I talk to him every day. I told you that in our last session."

"If I may ask, what are these conversations about between you and Satan?"

She half-smiled, "People in general being disobedient to him after all he has done for the majority!"

Mr. Silverman coughed and then cleared his throat. "Do you believe in God, Ms. Florence?"

Ms. Florence half-smiled once again. "That's a silly question. If you believe in one, you have to believe in the other one, Mr. Silverman."

Mr. Silverman rubbed his forehead like a scared little child. "Ms. Florence, who do you serve?"

"I serve the Devil. Who do you serve, Mr. Silverman?"

"I serve God, and you should, too, Ms. Florence!"

Suddenly, Mr. Silverman began to sweat profusely as if someone had thrown a bucket of water in his face.

Ms. Florence sat back on the couch and started laughing hysterically.

"What's wrong, Mr. Silverman; you starting to feel the heat from Hell?"

He stood up instantly from the couch and grabbed his briefcase and tape recorder. Then he headed toward the door. Before he reached the front door, he saw in front of him a huge, dark figure in the form of a man with a snake's face, and behind it stuck out a dragon's tail. It hissed at him with a fiery red tongue, and when it opened its eyes, they were dark red in color. Frightened to death, he ran past the figure out of the house into the open street, yelling for someone to help him. He ran directly into a bus moving at high speed, which hit him, causing him to fly several feet into midair, landing him on the hard concrete and splashing his brain matter all over the street.

Writing on the wall

From the strange homeless woman

If you believe in such an image

You will see such an image!

CHAPTER 5

Nine months later, the Philadelphia police authorities still had not found Melissa, so they labeled her as a missing person. A photo of her was put in every local store and pasted onto street poles throughout the entire neighborhood.

Richard and Dorothy were still traumatized over their son James' sudden death!

Alaysha was soon to give birth. The pain and the agony she endured in her belly made her yell out at times, "Get this piece of shit out of me!"

The doctors delayed the labor because a strange image showed up on ultrasound depicting a black and yellow baby ball python wrapped around the infant inside Alaysha's womb.

They were told later by the head doctor to go on with the procedure and deliver the infant. When Alaysha pushed out the infant, the doctors noticed that the baby ball python, which they had seen earlier on the ultrasound, had disappeared. When one of the doctors held the infant upside-down by both legs in mid-air, the infant showed no sign of breathing. So, he gently smacked the child's butt. He was startled when the infant's eyes opened halfway, appearing to be dark red in color, and then the eyes turned normal. Suddenly, chaos started to erupt in the hospital. The staff members began running around out of control like chickens with their heads cut off! Babies in every maternity ward were crying their lungs out while unborn babies in emergency rooms entered the world, busting out of their mothers' wombs. Some kicked foot-first out of their mothers' genital areas!

On that cloudy, gray day when the infant came into the world, people living in foreign countries cried tears of blood. Catherine and Alaysha were petrified when the lights went out. An unknown stranger dressed in black with his face concealed entered the room and snatched the infant from the doctor's arms and vanished into the hallway.

When the Man of God entered the front door of the hospital, the building shook a little. The voices he'd heard in his head went silent.

The following day, dead female bodies were removed from the emergency rooms of the hospitals. Over four hundred infants were missing, not only in Philadelphia, but in other cities around the country. Most hospitals were quickly abolished; paper reports and corpses were burned to a crisp!

Afraid of alarming the public and afraid it would have started a major catastrophe, the officials kept this a secret at the General Hospital in Philadelphia, Pennsylvania, in 1969.

The Man of God lost track that night. An invitation had been sent to him three days earlier that the Pope wanted to see him immediately. Little did he know it, but another young girl had suffered the same fate while giving birth to a child in Washington, D.C.!

Writing on the wall

From the strange homeless woman

The day will come when so many living

Will truly envy the dead!

CHAPTER 6

Six months went by, and Catherine still had heard nothing from her mother or even the whereabouts of her missing grandchild that had been kidnapped from the hospital.

The day that she and Alaysha returned home, they discovered that the house they once occupied had been burned down to the ground along with the neighboring house!

Ms. Florence's body was never recovered after the deadly fire. The only evidence found by law officials consisted of burned, cracked skeleton heads in different areas of the rubbish.

During the investigation, these human remains were found to have belonged to a number of missing people from the late fifties and the early sixties.

Melissa's decomposed body was discovered later; it had been mutilated. Since Ms. Florence's body had not been implicated in the fire, a warrant was issued for her arrest as well as warrants for Catherine and her daughter. So the two left Philadelphia in a hurry and moved to Baltimore, Maryland, with Catherine's younger half-sister, Tina.

Catherine never mentioned a word to Richard or Dorothy and left the couple worried and senseless!

Tina was an ambitious student who studied law and dreamed of working in the House of Congress someday. Her face saddened when Catherine told her the terrible news.

Catherine inhaled a deep breath and then blew it out slowly. "I really need to talk to a Catholic priest!"

"I'm a Baptist," laughed Tina.

Catherine stared at her sister in disgust and asked, "Since when?"

"Two years ago! Do you want to talk to my pastor?"

"I am Catholic, Tina!"

Tina swirled her head around and poked out her lips with her hands on her hips. "Whatever religion you serve does not matter. We are all from the same God!" she quipped.

Catherine rolled her eyes. "For someone that changes their religious belief as many times as you do, that's weird to say!" She agreed to meet her sister's pastor the following day.

Pastor Samuel, known as a God-fearing man in the community, was always preaching to people to get their house in order before the day of God's great wrath on Earth!

Catherine explained the same story to him that she had explained to her sister. "The doctor mentioned there was no penetration involved," she replied.

"What you are saying sounds unjustified within my belief," said Pastor Samuel.

Catherine angrily gritted her teeth, "You Baptist people don't believe in the supernatural."

Pastor Samuel shook his head in total disbelief. "The only woman I know who birthed a child without sexual contact was Mary, the Mother of Jesus Christ!"

As Catherine turned and began to walk away, he touched her lightly on her shoulder. "Please give me some time to talk to someone about this matter," he asked.

He also warned her not to mention a word to anyone until he contacted her to return to him.

Meanwhile, at the Vatican, the Pope told the Man of God about Catherine and that she may be aware of some vital information about the Infants. He had also had her followed since the day she and Alaysha had left the Vatican.

He received word from an archbishop in Baltimore that Catherine was seen on the south side entering the New Psalmist Baptist Church. They meditated for a while on the different voices in his mind, not knowing whether it was God or Satan. It began to irritate him.

After the meditation was over, he told the Pope that he had thought about stepping down from his position.

"Your successor has not been born. If you quit now, a curse will be upon your head. You cannot walk away from an assignment God has appointed you to," said the Pope.

"I am scared, Papa!" said the Man of God. "What if the wrong voice leads me astray again?"

The Pope put his arms behind his back and asked the Man of God to walk with him slowly down the hall.

"Men always hear voices from time to time, and evil thoughts come to mind often in these days and times. We inherit this through our being; we all have a purpose. Some are born to the ignorance of mankind! Deep inside, everyone knows right from wrong. Satan will attack you in so many ways. Like myself, you are a Man of God, and by being so, you will know the difference between the two."

After saying these words, the Pope dropped dead!

A large crowd of people surrounded the Vatican. They came from all around the world to bid their final goodbyes to the man who had been much loved and respected. The news said he died of a heart attack. The Man of God felt the Pope had been scared, concealing secrets from the world within the Vatican walls, secrets that may have killed him!

Writing on the wall

From the strange homeless woman

The day will soon come when the sky will turn black

And the moon will turn into blood!

CHAPTER 7

The day Catherine returned to her sister's house after the meeting with the pastor, Tina informed her that Alaysha had left, taking her clothing and did not return.

Tina opened a bottle of Chateau Lafite and poured some into separate wine glasses. Catherine swallowed the wine straight down and drank a second and third refill, and began to cry out loud. "First, my grandchild, then my mother, now my daughter—it's like they disappeared off the face of the Earth!"

Tina went for some tissues that had been stashed in her china cabinet and handed a few to her crying sister.

"This whole situation is weird," said Tina, setting down her glass of wine on the living room table. "I believe some supernatural twilight zone bullshit is going on!" She noticed Catherine needed a fourth refill, so she went back into the kitchen to retrieve another bottle. Then suddenly she heard a loud, banging sound coming from upstairs. Then she heard footsteps walking through the hallway.

Traumatized by the noise, she ran from her kitchen, dropping the bottle onto the floor where it shattered!

Catherine's eyes flew wide open in despair, "What's wrong?"

Startled, Tina began biting her nails. "Did you hear that noise?"

Catherine leaned over on the couch and laughed like a hyena. "You've had a little bit too much to drink, Tina."

Tina didn't pay Catherine any attention and went off upstairs to see who was invading her house. Her bedroom dresser had been turned over, with her important papers scrambled on the floor with drops of blood on them.

Eventually, Catherine, in a near-intoxicated state, caught up behind her. "My God, Tina, what happened?"

"This has been going on for a while, Catherine," said a stunned Tina. "Now that you mention it, I think we both need to see an ordained Priest!"

Catherine and Tina woke up the next day with distressing hangovers. The two had planned to visit Dorothy in Philadelphia until the Baltimore authorities could find a lead on Alaysha's whereabouts!

They attended a Catholic Church service before leaving, and Tina introduced Catherine to an old friend and priest she'd met some years ago when she was involved in the Catholic faith.

As Catherine began to tell her story once again to the priest, he instantly and frantically spoke in a loud rage while holding the Holy Bible firmly in his hand.

"You don't understand, Catherine, the day of reckoning is upon this whole nation. . . when woman will go against man, and evil will try to outdo good and only . . ."

His words came to a halt when a swarm of bees and ravens entered the church through the open windows. Tears of blood filled his eyes. He dropped the Bible from his hand and held his chest tightly, and then collapsed!

Fighting off the ravens and bees, Catherine and Tina headed for the exit. A group of people dressed in black with their faces concealed entered and grabbed them both and steered them outside into a black limousine that sped off down the street.

Writing on the wall

From the strange homeless woman

They say two will be born

Only one will rule!

CHAPTER 8

Dorothy had been reflective for some time now. Hearing nothing from Catherine made her life much more difficult.

Still in deep depression about his son's death, Richard had a heart attack and passed away not too long after Catherine had left.

She decided to travel to Georgia to catch up with an old voodooist friend called Witch Maggie! Not a living soul knew about Dorothy's involvement in witchcraft in her younger days when she was down on her luck.

This witch resided in the woods of the Deep South in Georgia. She'd helped a few movie stars, athletes, rock-and-roll band members, and even presidents to get elected in her younger days. Nowadays, only certain people know of her. She'd committed to herself to stay that way for numerous reasons. Witch Maggie's identity changed drastically. Her white hair had grown extremely long down to her buttocks.

Her face was concealed in pig's blood, and when she smiled, the veneers of her teeth were stained brown. Destined to be the greatest witch doctor of the South, she always wore a long, hooded black silk cape!

Bending down on her knees with her face pasted into the dirt, she felt a tap on her shoulder. She rose up off the ground like a robot.

She yelled excitedly, "What is it?"

Dorothy was stunned for a moment, and then she regained her composure. "It's me, Dorothy Brooks!"

Witch Maggie, looking not the least bit shocked, replied, "I remember you. Who can forget that face of a runaway Devil?"

Dorothy held her head down in a sudden, awkward position. "I'm really sorry, Maggie. I had to change my way of life!"

Witch Maggie gave her the sinister eye contact.

"Foolish nonsense. That is what they all say, but they always come back for help," she mumbled and groaned as she walked away from Dorothy.

"I really need your help!"

Witch Maggie stopped in her tracks. "Speak; I'm listening."

Dorothy told Maggie about Catherine and how her son had committed suicide. Witch Maggie suggested that Dorothy follow her into her tent, which was located in the dark parts of the woods.

"I'm sorry to hear about your son; you can't play in the Devil's playground and expect to walk out freely. Someone in your family had to pay the ultimate price!"

Those words, "Someone in your family had to pay the ultimate sacrifice," hit Dorothy in the chest like a thousand knives. She fell to her knees crying hysterically.

"Was it my fault my son died?"

"Yes, it was foolish, woman," answered Witch Maggie. "Now you are back again in the master's playground, ready to play again!"

"I don't want to play; I just want to know my friend's whereabouts!"

Witch Maggie laughed. "You are more foolish than I thought. When you come to visit me and step into this tent, you are ready to play."

She removed six black candles from her secret stash and set them on an old wooden table. She then asked Dorothy one more time if she still wanted to play.

While holding Dorothy's right hand up, Witch Maggie slid a small, sharp razor from underneath her tongue and sliced it across Dorothy's pinky finger. Dorothy moaned in a terrible sound. She held her pinky finger over each candle, watching closely as the blood dripped into each one. The candles were then lit. She sat down and offered Dorothy a seat where she would close her eyes to concentrate on her friend.

For a moment, everything seemed to be calm. Suddenly, Maggie leaped hysterically out of her chair. Dorothy's eyes opened wide. She stood up, stepped back, and became stunned by Maggie's reaction.

"I can't mess with them people; I'll be fighting Satan himself!" said Maggie.

"What people?" asked a paranoid Dorothy.

"I cannot mention their name, child. I'll be dead before dawn!"

A terrifying image appeared on Maggie's face. She hurried and blew out the candles and rushed out of the open tent with a frantic Dorothy following behind in her tracks.

"What do these people have to do with my friend?" asked Dorothy.

"I can't tell you, child. You have to get out of these woods!"

Dorothy gripped Maggie tightly by her arm. "Tell me, please!"

Maggie pushed Dorothy to the ground and began to back away slowly. "There is nothing to tell you. How do you think all them big-time politicians got their spot in Washington? I helped them, and I'm not ready to pay the piper!" She then turned around and ran farther into the deep, dark woods, leaving Dorothy on the ground in distress.

Writing on the wall

From the strange homeless woman

Laugh, my children, and play for now.

Soon it will be dawn, and playtime will be over!

CHAPTER 9

C atherine and Tina had been taken to an underground dwelling somewhere in South Carolina by an organization or cult of men and women called the Satanists. The hallways were long, dark, cold, and spooky with red lights and various images and pictures of Satan on the walls. In the middle of the floor stood a 206-foot tall, two-headed black snake statue with six dragon tails. People of every ethnic culture kneeled before this huge figure saying, "My god, my god; your children are safe!"

The women were told to kneel with the crowd. When Catherine refused, two women came from the crowd and pulled her down until both her knees touched the floor.

"Let go of my sister," yelled Tina, pushing one of the women down.

The other woman suddenly smacked Tina with her left hand.

Then a loud voice yelled out, "Enough! I'm sorry it came to this dreadful ending. You two would never understand."

The voice sounded so familiar; it was a voice they didn't want to believe. When the person unveiled her mask, Catherine and Tina almost fainted.

Tina's voice raged in fury, "You were always a sick, twisted bitch!"

The person laughed so loudly that it sent echoes throughout the underground place. "The Devil told me this was going to happen."

"And you say I'm the crazy one."

Ms. Florence snapped her fingers at a woman standing not too far from her. The woman was holding two infants wrapped in pure black silk sheets. When the woman removed the sheets from the two infants, they began to cry a demonic sound that frightened Catherine and Tina with a fear of the unknown!

Ms. Florence then gently took hold of one of the naked infants and shook it gently in front of her daughter's face.

"Catherine, this is your granddaughter. Her name is Lexia!" She then took hold of the other infant. "This is her brother, Luffa, from another mother!"

Catherine became instantly baffled. "What are you talking about, Mama?"

Ms. Florence's laugh echoed throughout the halls. "I guess you two have not heard the good news. These babies are Satan's twins!"

A crowd of men and women surrounded Catherine and Tina and started to sprinkle blood on them. When Tina reached out viciously, she was smacked in the face by one of the women. When Catherine tried to intervene, two men gripped her tightly.

"You two need to stop the drama," Ms. Florence yelled. "Your place is with us; this is Lucifer's world. You two better jump aboard!"

Catherine's weakened state would not allow her to pull away from the men who held her. So, she began to kick and yell out in the open air.

"This is God's world! God, not the Devil, built this entire world in six days and created everything on it!"

Ms. Florence ordered that they both be taken away. Before they were put into confinement, a terrified man with blood dripping from his mouth was dragged in front of them by force by two husky men. Ms. Florence began to explain his situation. "This is Senator Bob Wilson. He didn't want to accept that Satan is the true savior of this world. Instead, he said your god is the savior. So, I had my followers take a razor and cut his tongue out of his mouth. Now he can't speak—period!"

The senator was then dragged away.

Catherine cried profusely, "Why are you doing this to us?"

"You are doing this to yourself," replied Ms. Florence. "Wake up and smell Hell. You are in it!"

The automatic door shut tightly. As she limped down the narrow hallway, laughing and crying at the same time, the thought of going into Satan's eternal lake of fire often crossed Ms. Florence's mind.

She wondered at times if she'd made the right decision in choosing Satan over God. After all, Satan had given her a luxurious life in her younger days.

Now she started aging. Her face was wrinkled badly, not to mention the arthritis that claimed her body with every passing year of distress.

A succorer would be needed soon. Katie, a woman she chose from the occult group, started worshipping the Devil the same year she became the official leader.

Katie was ten years younger than Ms. Florence, and being ruler over the Satanists, she'd been the right candidate for the position!

Writing on the wall

From the strange homeless woman

Prepare for a war like never before.

Hell is upon us all!

CHAPTER 10
Five Years Later

Once a year in the spring, parents or legal guardians would unite with their children at this particular playground for certain games just to have fun. They would play soccer, baseball, basketball, jump rope, and hide-and-seek. This scene caught the eye of the twins, as playing as unattractive! They drifted off with a boy their age behind a sliding board while Katie wasn't paying them any attention.

Lexia whispered in an unknown tongue into Luffa's ear; he, in turn, whispered in an unknown tongue into the ear of a boy beside him. The whispering of the unknown tongue in one another's ears among the children went on throughout the entire playground. Suddenly, a little girl reached into a trash can for an empty glass bottle and smashed it on the ground. She ran towards her father and repeatedly jabbed the sharp, pointed edge into her father's stomach. Then all the children began attacking their parents with whatever objects they could find. There were screams of horror as the parents' heads were being bashed in with baseball bats, and they, too, were stabbed with sharp objects.

When the police arrived, they were even attacked.

"Officer down, officer down," a frightened officer yelled into his portable two-way radio when he was overtaken by a seven- and nine-year-old.

More children, even teenagers, entered the playground area. It became a blood bath for the first time in South Carolina! A call from the police district came across the radio to shoot to kill every child at that location. The twins stood in the midst and watched with smiles on their faces. Katie pulled them by their little arms and exited the playground. When the chaos was over, reporters were everywhere with their cameras, trying to find an eyewitness.

"The children were out of control!" A man recalled in front of the camera that he witnessed the chaos from a distance.

That evening, the Man of God heard of the terrible news. He returned to the Vatican to visit the newly assigned Pope. There were certain answers that needed to be addressed, and only the Pope could provide them. He was led by an archbishop to the Pope's secret chamber deep within the Vatican.

"I've been waiting for you. I knew you would come soon," said the Pope.

The Man of God sat down and took a deep breath. "I'm confused, Papa. I heard rumors buzzing around about the brother and sister taking control over the world!"

The Pope began to pour himself a stiff drink.

"Only one will take full control!"

As the Pope began to drink, the Man of God shook his head from side to side. "I can't comprehend what you are saying to me!"

"A spiritual battle from the depths of Hell has been lifted up here on Earth," replied the Pope as he placed his bottle on the table. He opened the drawer in front of him, pulled out a wrinkled, half-torn letter, and handed it to the Man of God. The Pope turned his head in silence.

The Man of God removed his eyeglasses from his top shirt pocket so that he could read the letter clearly. He tried to smooth out some of the wrinkles by rubbing them up and down on his right leg. The month, date, and year on the letter read November 30, 1969. He continued reading:

"I, Pope Matthew, finished eating my afternoon meal when I was led by the spirit to the Vatican Garden. What I saw with my own eyes almost blinded me. There, I saw two teenage girls, Alaysha and Amy, whom I knew well. They performed naked kissing and making out with one another. Then suddenly I fell backwards when I noticed a two-headed black snake come up from beneath the ground. One-bit Alaysha and the other bit Amy right in the middle of their stomachs! The two girls hurriedly began to dress. When it came time for the girls to return home, I, Pope Matthew, had them followed. They became pregnant instantly from the snake bites."

"Two hermaphrodite children were born from different mothers, one in Philadelphia, Pennsylvania, and one in Washington, D.C. It didn't matter what gender they became, but they were:
A boy named Luffa and
A girl named Lexia."

The letter fell from his hand onto the floor.

"How long have you known, Papa?" asked the Man of God.

"The first day the College of Cardinals chose me!"

The Man of God suddenly became saddened. So, the two are from different Mothers.

"How will I know which one will rule?"

The Pope walked towards him and extended his right hand over his white veil. "Only the one who takes power over all nations!"

The Man of God bowed his head and kissed the Pope's hand. He raised his head, and in his eyes was an ocean full of tears. He held firmly both of the Pope's hands. "Power over you, too?" asked the Man of God.

"Yes, I'm afraid so," answered the Pope.

Writing on the wall

From the strange homeless woman

Foolish people, why make a promise

You can't keep?

CHAPTER 11

The Man of God was led a month later to travel to Baltimore, Maryland, to connect with an old-time friend, Pastor Samuel. He was sent by a holy spirit.

As soon as the Man of God stepped off the plane, a weird, possessed man spat directly in his face.

"You bastard, stay away!" The man hurried down the street into an open crowd.

His flesh rendered him almost fearful until his spirit within enlightened him to fear only God. The Man of God checked himself into a nearby motel in the downtown area and caught up with Pastor Samuel the next morning in a secluded part of Druid Hill Park. As they began their conversation, six husky demonic pit bulls came out of nowhere and surrounded them. The dogs barked and gnashed and grit their sharp teeth as red saliva dripped out of their mouths.

The Man of God took a firm hold of his cane and smacked it down on the ground.

"In the name of God, Satan, let thee be!" he yelled.

And in the quick flash of a moment, the dogs vanished.

"We have to leave this park," mumbled the Man of God. "It is the Devil's playground. What people do in this park is an abomination in the sight of God's eyes! We have to go to a sacred place.!"

Not too far from the park Alaysha was being baptized at Saints Philip and James Catholic Church. She was about to become a nun. When she left her mother and her aunt Tina some years ago, she chose to live a celibate life. Now becoming a nun, her everyday schedule would involve a lot of hours in contemplation with God.

The people she met and stayed with for a short time were of the Catholic faith and believed it would be essential for her to become a nun after she told them her story of what happened at the Vatican and her mysterious pregnancy. After her confirmation of the baptism, Alaysha noticed a woman sitting in one of the back pews with her head down. She was sobbing.

Alaysha politely handed the woman a napkin and asked the lady what the problem was. When the woman raised her head and sniffed her nose, Alaysha's eyes widened. "Ms. Dorothy!" she whispered softly.

Dorothy rose and embraced Alaysha tightly in her arms. She pushed her back a little and stared her up and down. "It's so good to see you, Alaysha, after all these years!"

Although Alaysha wore a coif and a veil, she was still recognizable, having that same little-girl face.

"How is your mother?" asked Dorothy bluntly.

Alaysha bowed her head in total silence.

A blind man appeared and intervened before she could say another word. He spoke with an eerily pitched voice, "She is captured in the bottom south where no true believer of Jesus will enter alone!"

Then his reflection became blurry in their eyesight, and he slowly disappeared. They both rubbed their eyes in disbelief, and not long after that occurred, Alaysha excommunicated herself from nun duties to go on a search with Dorothy to look for her mother and other kin folks or relatives.

Writing on the wall

From the strange homeless woman

They say a New World Order Is coming like never before.

Whoever thought the price over

Our heads would be so high?

CHAPTER 12

Alaysha had been awakened by a beam of sunlight shining through an open curtain and the smell of freshly brewed coffee. A note from Dorothy lay on the motel nightstand. It read: "Went out for breakfast."

When she finally got her vision together, Alaysha noticed a woman standing over her. The woman appeared as a solid, hard, muscle-bound man with a torn half T-shirt showing her ripped abs and a butch haircut. It was Amy, the person she had so sexually indulged herself with at the Vatican when they were teenagers.

Amy leaned down and gently squeezed Alaysha's arms.

When Amy tried to French-kiss her, Alaysha pushed her away, and with piercing eyes stared the woman up and down.

"How did you know I was here, and why are you in Baltimore?" asked Alaysha.

Amy leaned against the wall and pulled a cigarette from her top shirt pocket.

"I have some news about your mother," Amy said after lighting her cigarette.

Still stressed at the horror going on in her life, Alaysha began rubbing her stomach in a circular motion. It had been absolutely clear she hadn't eaten.

Amy watched her facial expression as it changed periodically. When Alaysha's stomach continued to growl, they decided to go out to eat and get caught up with one another. They rode on Amy's motorcycle to the nearest restaurant that served breakfast and lunch.

When the waiter handed them a menu, they ordered a medium-rare steak, mashed potatoes, with steamed broccoli. Alaysha noticed Dorothy eating at the table across from them.

"I assumed you were happy to see me," said Amy, staring nervously out the window.

"A little. How come you seem paranoid?" asked Alaysha.

A waiter came and gently set their plates and drinks on the table and walked away.

Amy started the conversation about Alaysha's grandmother, Ms. Florence, being a cult leader, and both their mothers being held prisoner and their children sent to Georgia to unite with another cult.

Alaysha was astonished to hear that Amy had also given birth to a child.

For a moment, they both were bewildered about how they had become pregnant at the same time until it finally crossed their minds that it must have been that two-headed snake bite.

Amy noticed six elderly men were watching her closely from outside the restaurant. She quickly handed Alaysha a card that read: "Hell's Gate Oakwood Cemetery, Spartanburg, South Carolina." She kissed Alaysha on the cheek and hurried off to her motorcycle and rode carelessly down the street while the six men followed behind in a black van.

Alaysha was baffled about what she had just heard and seen. She nervously began biting her fingernails until Dorothy warned her by surprise!

"Have you finished eating?"

Alaysha moved her fingers slowly from her lips and muttered. "I think so."

Dorothy went into a sudden tantrum by smacking both her ears. Since she'd visited Witch Maggie and had committed to play with the Devil, she had been hearing demonic voices in her head, whispering awful things to make her feel uneasy.

Alaysha stared at her in disbelief. "Are you all right, Ms. Dorothy?"

Dorothy sat down and held Alaysha's hand firmly. "I have something to tell you."

"Tell me what—Ms. Dorothy?"

Dorothy began to tell the story about her witchcraft days and even about Witch Maggie and thinking that perhaps she could help them.

Although Alaysha now knew the whereabouts of her mother and her aunt Tina, she still wanted to travel to Georgia to meet Witch Maggie. Late in the evening, they boarded the Amtrak train to Savannah, Georgia. When Dorothy returned, Witch Maggie was waiting patiently in her tent for their arrival.

"I knew you would return, child, even with a friend."

She sprinkled some black dust on the ground, which she had removed from a brown pouch.

Dorothy stood shivering, drenched in sweat.

"What did you do to me?"

"I didn't do nothing; you did it yourself," said Witch Maggie sarcastically.

"Did what to myself? I came here asking for help to find my friend. Now I'm hearing weird things."

An angry expression appeared on Witch Maggie's face. She banged her tight, hard fist on the table.

"When you stepped into this tent, you swore allegiance with the Devil!"

51

"I never swore allegiance to the Devil!" yelled Dorothy.

Witch Maggie sat in a wooden rocking chair in the corner of the tent and giggled.

"You are an old fool; you people make me laugh, coming to me asking for certain help. When you come to me, you make bargains with the Devil!"

She leaped from the chair and took hold of Dorothy and Alaysha's hands and led them into the deep, dark part of the woods.

"Where are you taking us"? asked Alaysha as she nearly fell over a tree branch.

"Hush, child, the demons will hear you!"

Witch Maggie let go of their hands and began speaking in an unknown tongue.

Alaysha shook with fright when Witch Maggie burst out loud: "I AM!"

"I AM!" asked surprised Dorothy.

"The Child of Satan, the ruler of this entire world!"

Witch Maggie then ran further into the woods, leaving Dorothy clueless. She had been cursed; so had some officials in high offices. A few didn't know; the minority didn't give a damn! Sooner or later, they would have to pay the piper.

Witch Maggie knew the rules to the game. She even knew not to go against a force that would rip her soul apart in Hell!

Writing on the wall

From the strange homeless woman

Some walls can talk

If you listen quietly!

CHAPTER 13

When Alaysha and Dorothy arrived at Hell's Gate Oakwood Cemetery, the place was desolate with broken pieces of headstones scattered about after a war between the Satanists and another cult organization. Their underground dwelling had been vandalized. They quickly relocated to the Black Forest in Germany. A few residents called it a sanctuary for the abnormal. After being watched under close scrutiny by the German authorities, they then traveled back to the United States to Savannah, Georgia's Forsythe Park, where they remained hidden until the twins had become teenagers.

Lexia grew to be very beautiful, with radiant skin and long, silky black hair. She attended Savannah High School. Most female students were jealous. Some were hypnotized by her beauty! She was ambitious, had a very high IQ, and was number one on the girls' basketball team. And when singing and dancing, she was brilliant.

Luffa possessed the same talents. He was 5'6" with a muscular build and very handsome. He attended Miller's Preparatory Academy School for Boys in Lithonia, Georgia.

Despite being twins, they had no love for each other, so Ms. Florence separated them. When Lexia graduated, she attended the Atlanta Metropolitan State College. Luffa left the cult without saying a word.

At age twenty-three, Lexia felt she did not need approval from the cult members. Ms. Florence became overly cautious for her safety. She warned Lexia that various people were searching for her, seeking to know her whereabouts as well as Luffa's.

Ms. Florence died before she could give Lexia additional information.

"The Devil told me this was going to happen, and they always thought I was the crazy one!" Those were the last words that came out of Ms. Florence's mouth.

Lexia took Ms. Florence's warnings seriously, so she disguised herself on most occasions, especially when she traveled to foreign countries.

While in China, she received a telegram at the Beijing Marriott Hotel from an unknown Russian male asking her to meet him at the Kempinski Hotel. At that time, she had forgotten about the warning, and she took the next flight to Russia.

Two men accompanied her from the Moscow Sheremetyevo Airport to the Kempinski Hotel. To her surprise, there sat Luffa in plain view as they were entering the vestibule.

"My dear, lovely sister, I'm so honored you could make it!"

He kneeled down and kissed her hand.

"So, this is where you hide from the world," said Lexia as she was being seated by the two men.

"Just staying out of the way," he laughed.

Luffa had become filthy rich and thus a powerful prince of a secret society that preyed on animals in satanic rituals.

He asked his secret agents to accompany him and his sister to a private room. When left alone, they made eye contact and began to feel sexual desire for each other.

He held Lexia desperately in his arms. His tongue excited her mouth as a roaring snake in motion, touching her warm, sensitive lips.

She grabbed him by his private parts, tore his pants open, and pushed him onto the bed. She ripped her blouse open, revealing her breasts, and then plunged them into his mouth. Within seconds, she was on top of him like she was riding a black stallion! A rage of fire came from underneath them. Then, in the throes of their passion, a huge, two-headed snake wrapped around them with rapid speed.

Ten midget demons appeared and played merry-go-round. There were moaning noises and demonic screams. Within ten minutes, it was over!

Writing on the wall

From the strange homeless woman

In the Devil's eyes

Evil is Good!

CHAPTER 14

Pastor Samuel finished his evening service and prepared himself to go home. When interrupted by one of the choir singers, he reopened the church and led the young lady into the sanctuary. She sat down in the first pew and stared maliciously at him.

"I always had feelings for you. Is that wrong?"

Pastor Samuel felt a little uncomfortable when sitting down.

"It is nothing wrong to have affection for someone. As you know, I am a man of the cloth."

She gradually glided over toward him and started to unzip her jacket.

"What are you doing, young lady?" he asked nervously, rising quickly to his feet when she aroused his pelvic area.

She pulled him back onto the bench, ripped her skirt open, and then jumped on his lap and wrapped her legs around his waist.

"It will feel so good if you were inside me!"

"Get off me!" he yelled.

He tried to push her off his lap. She snatched the gold cross chain from around his neck and jabbed the cross piece into both of his eyes. She then leapt down off him like a frog and bounded out of the church. The Man of God entered the sanctuary and watched the blood squirt out of Pastor Samuel's eyes.

"I can't see," Pastor Samuel began to scream horrifically. "My god, I can't see!"

The sounds of sirens coming from police vehicles caught the attention of the possessed young woman, leaping down the street like a frog going crazy. She leapt onto one of the vehicles and was shot multiple times.

The Man of God followed behind paramedics to a nearby hospital. He knew the attack on the pastor was done by an evil spirit from Hell waiting to torment living souls.

When the deacon of the church heard the terrible news on television, he hurried to the hospital. Pastor Samuel's face was badly swollen. He placed his hand in the pastor's hand and squeezed it tightly.

"It's me, Deacon Johnson."

Pastor Samuel moved his head side to side. He was irritable for a moment. "I never believed in demonic possession," he said angrily. "The woman was possessed!"

Deacon Johnson stared up at the ceiling. "What are you saying?"

"The way she removed her clothing, she jumped on me like something from Hell."

The Man of God noticed tears trickling from beneath the bandage that covered the pastor's eyes.

"I feel your spirit is deeply hurt!"

The pastor sat up and wiped his face. "There are words I can't speak; I'm so ashamed."

The Man of God set his cane against the wall and sat on the right side of the pastor. "You don't have to be ashamed, my friend. You are only human."

"I lied to my congregation," said Pastor Samuel in rage. "I kept nasty thoughts of her in my mind. She played them out!"

A nurse entered and asked for privacy. When the two left the room, the nurse shut the door and pulled down the shade.

Deacon Johnson and the Man of God went outside for sixty seconds to confer on the pastor's condition. After hearing a scream, they returned to the room and saw a staff member running out of the room to alarm other staff members that someone had strangled the pastor to death!

The day after Lexia and Luffa were sexually involved, a legion of demons came up from Hell and spread like a pandemic around the world, causing people to indulge in various acts of sin. The Pope at that time knew it was the beginning of Hell's birth pains!

Writing on the wall

From the strange homeless woman

When they have your mind

Set on one situation

They are behind private doors

Doing something in secret!

CHAPTER 15

The Man of God knew that eventually he would have to return to the Vatican and explain to the Pope about the spiritual warfare that was underway in the United States.

He flew in a private jet to Rome. While inflight in his mind he went into a frightful hallucination of a huge, two-headed black snake with demonic eyes and hissing its fiery tongue at him. He grabbed his chest tightly and made a terrifying scream.

A stewardess came along and placed her hand on his shoulder. "Are you all right, sir?"

"Yes," he answered, breathing hard.

He asked the stewardess for a drink of water. As she walked away, he reached for a napkin from his pocket and wiped the sweat off his forehead. Then it happened again. When he glanced out the rear window, in his view the entire world was on fire. He placed both hands over his eyes and then took a peek between his fingers. This time everything down on Earth seemed normal.

The Pope awaited his arrival in one of the Vatican's secret rooms. The Man of God entered with an abnormal appearance. He kneeled down and ceremoniously kissed the ring on the third finger of the Pope's right hand.

"Why have you stayed away so long, my friend," asked the Pope.

He raised his head and stared softly into the Pope's eyes. "I was afraid death would follow."

"Death comes with you or without you; it needs no invitation," replied the Pope.

The Man of God stood up from his knees and began to smear his hands across the wall. "There are secrets within these Vatican walls that must be exposed, Papa!"

The Pope whispered politely in his ear. "The truth must always stay hidden from the world."

"What is the truth?" the Man of God whispered back in curiosity.

The Pope walked over and opened the door for the Man of God to exit. "You cannot know the truth until the time comes!"

The Man of God left the Vatican in distress. He returned to the United States under severe stress, causing him to faint. When he regained consciousness, a woman more beautiful than the midnight stars and with a voice as lovely as an angel stood over him. She helped him up with her kindness and welcomed him into her home.

She held him in her arms and began to nurse a small bruise on his forehead, a bruise sustained in a bad fall he had taken. She offered him a drink of alcohol and sex. He refused both. His status with God had always been close. The next morning, when he opened his eyes, breakfast had been set before him in bed. He noticed a note on the side of the tray that read: "I'll see you at the appointed time of your death!"

Writing on the wall

From the strange homeless woman

Think before you react.

Who knows what tomorrow may bring!

CHAPTER 16

Still unaware of the truth of what had happened, Alaysha came to the realization that her mother and aunt were dead.

Catherine and Tina had been confined in separate, isolated rooms without windows for thirteen years. They never acknowledged the light of day. They didn't know the days, months, or years.

Their rooms had a terrible scent of pure funk from their dried feces and urine on the floor. Catherine's hair grew wildly down her back; Tina's fingernails also grew extremely long. They were given small amounts of food from time to time and little water to keep them barely alive. Catherine would cry when she heard the door latch unlock.

"Please help me, Mama!"

Ms. Florence stood over her, tapping one bare foot on the floor, contemplating. "Are you ready to jump onboard with us?" she asked politely.

Catherine burst angrily into more tears. "I'll never take sides with the Devil!"

At the time, Ms. Florence grinned. "You will eventually, or you will stay in this room until your God comes. That is what they teach you?"

Dorothy and Alaysha returned to Hell's Gate Oakwood Cemetery in Spartanburg, South Carolina.

Frantically, Alaysha had been staying in different hotels. Dorothy then came up with the plan for them to begin doing a little witchcraft on their own.

"The only way to defeat evil is to create a delusion."

They settled out into the deep part of the cemetery and began to burn black candles and even stripped a couple of homeless black cats they'd found on the open road, a ritual she had learned from Witch Maggie.

They even went so far as to remove dirt from the cemetery ground and made it into a decoction and watched one of Satan's advocates appear in the mist. When they saw a huge black two-headed snake come roaring through the mist, slashing at them, they ran out of the cemetery and hitch-hiked a ride back to the hotel. With a hostile attitude, Alaysha slammed the car door quite forcefully.

"Are you crazy? You cannot serve two masters!"

The conversation escalated into an argument between the two, and then suddenly, a white limousine came to a screeching halt.

A thin man opened the door and yelled for them to get in quickly. They ignored him for a short moment until they realized a group of people with demonic eyes had come running out of the hotel toward them.

The chauffeur pressed down hard on the gas pedal!

A dark mist of fog from the limousine's exhaust pipe shrouded the group. When the fog cleared, the group of people had disappeared.

The thin man slid over and introduced himself as a messenger from the divine. "It has been a long time, Dorothy," he said.

Dorothy squinted her eyes, staring at him in curiosity. "Excuse me!"

"You were nine at the time," said the messenger, taking her by the hand and holding it gently. "A bad seed was given to you from someone sinister. At the time, your mother was told to abort the child by me and my colleagues. The child would have grown to have mental issues."

Dorothy was lost for words, and then broke out of her silence. "How come I don't remember?"

"You were under a satanic spell for a period of time. Since a child, you were hypnotized by a secret society and affiliated with your mother in worshipping the Devil."

"What secret society?" Alaysha interrupted.

"There are a lot of secret societies in this world," the thin man whispered. He paused for a moment and then continued speaking slowly.

"Dorothy, your mother was captive under Satan's teaching and followed the doctrine. That is why when you became a fully grown adult, it was easy for you to do rituals with that witch!"

Dorothy was surprised this stranger knew about her mother's past history and her dealings with Witch Maggie. The thought of her having a child before James was absurd.

"If you are truly a messenger from the divine, where is my mother?" asked Alaysha, staring deeply into his cloudy eyes.

He turned his face slightly away from hers. "I know nothing about your mother. What I do know is you gave birth to one of Lucifer's twins."

Puzzled at the words that exited his mouth, Alaysha expressed her annoyance with a squint of her eyes. When the limousine came to a sudden stop, the chauffeur escorted them onto the sidewalk.

"That's it?" asked Dorothy fiercely. "You feed me this nonsense. I was pregnant at nine, not to mention my friend's daughter birthed a child from Hell."

The messenger stepped out of the limousine and rested each hand on Dorothy and Alaysha's shoulders.

"You two will find the answers to your questions soon." He turned to step back into the limousine. Dorothy gripped his arm.

"Who is this man that impregnated me?"

The messenger turned away and stared up at the sky. "Satan is playing this everlasting game with people's souls," said the messenger. "Thinking that will never end, but in every beginning, just as we were born, there will be an ending," continued the messenger.

He warned them both to hide underground with the mole people until it was safe to resurface. He also explained that the people who had run out of the hotel towards them were possessed by demonic spirits. They took his advice and hid from the brutal world.

At times, Alaysha would go into deep thought about her mother, grandmother, and her aunt Tina, but most of all, she thought of Amy and the child she had birthed.

How did this catastrophe start in the first place, and who's been the mastermind behind it? She knew now it didn't begin with her love affair with Amy when they were teenagers. The picture was much bigger!

Writing on the wall

From the strange homeless woman

A legion from Hell is coming.

Be prepared to fight in this Demonic battle!

CHAPTER 17

The twenty-first century had begun. It was the start of a new millennium! Witch Maggie had died of a sudden heart attack a year earlier at the age of ninety-eight. Politicians and big-name movie stars attended the funeral service. When laid to rest, her headstone read:

"Witch Maggie May.

To those I helped to their fortune and fame—see you in Hell!"

Luffa had finally come out of concealment from his underground society. He transferred from Russia to California and mysteriously became governor. He contributed millions of dollars to the general board of education, and he even hired a construction crew to build new homes for low-income people. He went so far as to help individuals pay off serious debts!

Lexia worked as a community activist in Washington, D.C., helping with environmental causes and making improvements in the society for women. She believed the time had come for women to take charge, not to sit in the house washing dishes or changing wet diapers. Women were supposed to be the head, not the tail!

In one of her speeches, she kindly expressed that women mature faster than men. So, whoever came up with the idea that men should be in charge failed to understand reality. Women took heed to this message and began to run for city councils, governorships, mayoral contests, and even United States Senators. This started chaos in the houses of Congress when men were being pushed aside. She sat among the homeless, giving them food and shelter in many states. When asked

73

by a local Philadelphia news reporter, "Why are you so gracious?" she replied:

"The greatest commandment of all is to love one another!"

When Luffa heard of all the good his sister was doing, he planned a meeting at the Santa Clara Center, telling everyone that in years to come, he would run for president of the United States of America! Lexia told her colleagues the same thing.

After a while, the two (Lexia and Luffa) went on separate vacations in Paris and met each other at the Michelin Star Restaurant.

"My dear, lovely sister, it is a pleasure to see you again," said Luffa as he kissed his sister on the cheek and offered her a seat.

Lexia sat with her legs crossed. She lit a cigarette and then blew smoke in his face. He fanned the wafting smoke with his hand and smiled like a child seeing Santa Claus for the first time.

"I heard a strange rumor you're running for president."

She rolled her head in a circular motion, cracking the bones in her neck, and asked, "What is it to you?"

Luffa went into a hysterical tantrum. He wanted to grip her neck and squeeze tightly until her eyes popped.

"Are you out of your mind? You're supposed to follow me!"

The yelling caught the attention of the other patrons. Lexia's antics became even more outrageous when she flicked her cigarette on the floor and stumped it.

"You men can't even control your own balls, let alone the government. It is a woman's turn now to show men how shit is done!"

"Ms., what are you doing?" asked a nearby waiter. "It is prohibited to stump a cigarette on the floor!"

"Burn in hell!" she yelled at the waiter. As she got up from her seat to walk to the front door, she paused and then turned and watched the waiter screaming and running throughout the burning restaurant.

Luffa ran and caught up with Lexia on the outside before she could open the door to her car.

"Lexia," he whispered closely but loud enough so she could hear him, "Have you forgotten we are cut from the same cloth? You will listen and obey me!"

Lexia pushed him away, got into her car, and slammed the door. When the automatic window lowered, she spat on him.

"Not a chance in Daddy's Hell!" The wheels on her silver Porsche squeaked as she backed up and pulled off.

Writing on the wall

From the strange homeless woman

If you're not living right,

Beware of the star that twinkles at night!

INTERMISSION

CHAPTER 18

Carl Willingham, a dynamic evangelist speaker in Washington, D.C., held a free church revival at Walter E. Washington Convention Center. The Man of God had been accompanied in a wheelchair by a group of religious leaders. There were various religious beliefs among the people in the building. There were Baptists, Catholics, Muslims, Jehovah's Witnesses, Israelites, Pentecostals, and even Seventh Day Adventists. There were monks and many others who congregated to hear about the coming of the one that claimed to be I AM.

"Who is this person?" shouted someone in the crowd. "He is a man with the number 666," yelled Carl into the microphone.

"This man that claims he is the Savior has already come into this world to deceive many! Do not be fooled by his generous giving and handsome smile. Behind that smile is a treacherous man that will lead your soul straight to Hell!" There was loud laughter and conversation among the crowd of people. Then someone yelled out loud, "You might be him!"

Some people laughed. The leaders were concerned, while others grew worried.

"Please don't be ignorant," said Carl. "Don't you people think the world has been ignorant enough?"

Just then, Alaysha and Dorothy entered the building. The underground dwelling where they hid had little food and drinking water. Since there were more children than adults, the children had first priority. One evening, Dorothy sensed something amiss in the atmosphere and began to pull on Alaysha's shirt.

79

"I'm scared!"

Alaysha's face had a puzzled appearance. "You don't have to be scared; we are perfectly safe," she stated.

When they saw flashlights flashing and heard the loud noise of military soldiers running throughout the underground dwelling, they moved to another location and came across a Shaman couple. For eight years, Keith and Linda Scott had frequently practiced a method of physical healing. But when they witnessed a man coming out of his skin and showing his true identity as a demon, they were traumatized.

"What in the world is going on?" a shivering Dorothy asked.

The chaos quieted down; then they heard a match strike in the middle of the darkness. Several men and women stood in a circle holding hands. One woman extended her arm out toward them.

"Come, pray with us!" she said.

Suddenly, they heard an outburst from a man pleading for his life and a deep voice yelling like a lieutenant in the army.

"What is your religious belief?"

"I'm a Christian!" replied a crying man.

There were multiple gunshots fired. Afterwards, they heard people running throughout the darkness like scavengers looking for food. Alaysha took a firm hold of Dorothy, saying, "We have to move now!"

Keith and Linda stayed behind with the prayer warriors. More gunshots rang out after Alaysha and Dorothy were a mile away. They returned to the surface and hijacked an oncoming car from a nervous elderly couple, and on to the nearest highway, they headed towards Washington, D.C.

The Man of God rolled his wheelchair up the ramp onto the stage. He gently removed the microphone from Carl's hand and asked the crowd to calm down. He cleared his throat and began to speak.

"I believe we will find out soon. I pray to God we're not too late."

Alaysha excused herself to visit the bathroom. While staring in the mirror, the grief struck her instantly. In her head, she felt her mind spin around like a Ferris wheel. She punched the mirror with her bare fist when she saw the image of her face as a demon.

"I, myself, have been searching for this person for many years. Still to this day, I have no clue about the identity of this individual. What I do know is that these twins were born in the year of nineteen hundred sixty-nine from two different young girls—a boy and a girl—one in Philadelphia, the other child in Washington, DC. Now, which one claims to be the Savior? We still don't know the answer to that question as of yet!"

Someone knocked on the door. "Are you all right?" a voice yelled from the other side of the door.

"I'm all right," she mumbled. She hurriedly wiped the blood drops off the sink with a wad of toilet paper wrapped around her fist and exited the bathroom. She joined with Dorothy in the midst of the crowd, unaware that the Man of God was staring at her from a distance. He quickly rolled his wheelchair down the ramp over to where she stood and began to cry.

"Alaysha, my child, I've been searching for you for so many years!"

Stunned, Alaysha stared at the crippled man in dismay. "Excuse me. Do I know you?" she inquired.

Dorothy, terrified to death, held Alaysha tightly by her arms.

"There is no reason to be frightened. I know the history of you and Amy!"

A lot of whispering went on among the religious leaders as they closely watched Alaysha and Dorothy. The Man of God began to feel tension in the air.

Accompanied by three religious leaders and Carl, he had them follow him outside the convention center and into a parked van.

Night came as daylight went. The seven of them checked into a double-size room at a Loew's Hotel. Upon entering, the staff members stared strangely at them. After announcing an impending visit to see the Pope the following day, the Man of God fell sound asleep.

Dorothy paced the floor back and forth while Alaysha watched her closely.

"You need to get some sleep," she said.

"I can't sleep with all this confusion going on," replied Dorothy.

One of the religious leaders put his hand on Dorothy's shoulder. "There is no reason to fear; the Lord has us in his hands!"

Carl then took hold of her and sat her down politely.

"You've touched the Devil; didn't you, Dorothy?"

"I didn't mean to!"

"I touched him, too," Alaysha interrupted. "Now I have to get my soul back from that bastard!"

Carl asked them both if they believed in God. They both nodded their heads—yes.

A rock suddenly shattered the glass window. The room went pitch black and cold.

They heard a deep, loud voice from the Man of God. "Don't speak of God in this room. What people did in this room is an abomination in the sight of God's eyes. We must leave this room!"

Instead of relocating to another hotel, the six caught the next plane to Rome to visit the Pope. The Pope had them sit in his private chamber, and he began to tell the story of the past men that had taken office as an archbishop, of which there had been many before his time. There was one particular archbishop who thought he was God himself and started lurking on the dark side. Unaware of the consequences, his mind had transformed; also, his spirit within his flesh became evil! He sexually assaulted young boys and girls, even murdered some of them if they indicated they would tell. There were letters found about Dorothy's mother and Ms. Florence—both Devil worshippers. Also, there were letters from her mother about Dorothy's sacrifice to the Devil at the age of nine, having sex with the archbishop, and then returning to live a luxurious lifestyle. Some mentioned the infant she'd given birth to, which somehow survived its own death and is still living this day.

"Stop this foolish talk. You expect me to believe those lies?" yelled Dorothy in rage.

"There are no lies permitted in this sacred place," said the Pope.

Dorothy burst into tears, "A boy or a girl?"

The Pope reached down into his robe and pulled out a picture, and handed it to Dorothy.

"This is your son. His name is Tillman!"

In total shock, Dorothy covered her mouth with her hand. "My son, where is my son?"

The Pope took a deep breath. "The last time I was told he was with the Illuminati, maybe the freemasons or the elite!"

Alaysha was saddened by what she heard. She held her head down and began to wipe the falling tears from her eyes. The Pope walked slowly towards her. He leaned down and whispered softly in her ear. "I cannot judge you; only God can judge you. I only pray you've put away childish things!"

He then turned towards the Man of God, "Any word on the twins?"

"I still don't have a clue, Papa," answered the Man of God.

They were led out by the Pope and his right-hand man. The three religious leaders stayed behind in the Vatican while the rest of them returned to the United States of America.

Writing on the wall

From the strange homeless woman

Always stay righteous

With the Lord

For your reward will be

Magnificent in Heaven!

CHAPTER 19

The year two thousand and one is a year the World will never forget because of the attacks on the World Trade Center in New York City and the Pentagon. That year is also memorable because of the Oklahoma City bombing and the people that died in a violent earthquake in India.

The years flew by quickly; so, did each presidential term. In the year 2020, everyone hoped for the best, which only turned out to be the worst when a pandemic came along and spread around the entire globe, killing millions! Social media became the life of some people. Their cell phones became god-like in their hands. A new president had been elected. Then, four years later, the time came again to elect a new president!

Dorothy and Alaysha returned to their hometown. Their neighborhood had changed drastically throughout the years. They were still being followed now and then. So, they decided to return to Washington, D.C. and check back into the motel where Carl had been staying for the moment.

"What's the plan?" asked Carl, as he lay across his bed twiddling his thumbs.

"I really don't have one. I know we can't hide forever," smiled Alaysha.

Dorothy sat down on the bed across from Carl, nodding her head up and down as a sign of disgust. "I spent my entire life savings!"

Suddenly, they heard a growling and scratching sound at the window. Alaysha was stunned when Carl got up from the bed and started walking toward the window.

"Carl, what are you doing?"

Respectfully, he signaled to Alaysha to hush, while Dorothy started biting her nails. He pulled back the curtains, and in minutes the glass shattered. A demonic German shepherd crashed in and bit Carl's throat, holding in its jaws Carl's entire throat cavity.

Dorothy began screaming and running behind Alaysha in fear for her life. Alaysha stared the dog in his eyes as he moved forward towards them, gnashing his teeth, until luckily the motel owner entered and fired off a single shot with his shotgun. The dog scampered out of the room and vanished into the midnight.

"What the hell happened here?" asked the owner, who was visibly shaken and suspicious of what had been taking place in the room.

Alaysha glanced down at the lifeless body of Carl as the blood poured heavily from his gaping throat. She then fled from the room with Dorothy in hand, yelling for a cab. Neither of them had a cell phone to call for a taxi. It started to pour down rain; then lightning flashed throughout the skies to the sound of thunder. They were soaked and wet when they finally caught a ride.

"What are we going to do now?" asked Dorothy, looking terrified as ever. "We don't have any money for a motel."

As always, Alaysha turned and smiled, adding, "Back underground until we figure this out!"

Sadly, Dorothy stared out the car window at the drizzling rain. "I was afraid you would mention something of that fact!"

The next morning in Washington, D.C., a fleet of limousines lined up in front of a secluded building. Led by ushers, a crowd of people dressed in black entered a huge auditorium.

"AM Not"

State Senator Robert Vowell and Congresswoman Mary McGraw addressed the many issues affecting the American people. Everyone sat quietly when Lexia ostentatiously walked down the aisle wearing a tight purple skirt outfit. Two ushers helped her on the stage. After giving the audience a half-hearted smile, she nudged Mary McGraw aside and grabbed hold of the microphone. "I will be one of the candidates running for president in the 2028 election!"

"So you say!" said Senator Robert Vowell.

"What party, dear?" asked Mary McGraw.

Lexia flung back her long, silky hair.

"I would say neither, but I have to play fair by the rules in playing this so-called game of politics!"

Mary McGraw was a short, feisty woman with a squeaky voice, and when she asked a question, she wanted a definite answer right away.

"You have to let your associate know. Anyway, it is quite brutal for a woman to run for president in these days and times. After all, this is a man's world!"

Lexia let out a devious laugh and winked her eye. "Maybe now," she replied.

"Count me in, too," yelled a voice from the back of the room. Luffa stood with his Secret Service men. "I also will be running in the 2028 election!"

Lexia seemed alarmed by his presence. She smiled at him in dismay. "Are you serious?"

"Yes, my sister," he said as he walked down the aisle alone and snapping his fingers. "I'm serious as diabetes, cancer, AIDS, COVID-19, and all those deadly, man-made diseases!"

Lexia walked off the stage and stood face-to-face with him as always, saying, "If you want to roll the dice, you'd better roll them right. Just remember my number—666!"

She shoved him aside and continued walking toward the exit.

Luffa laughed and yelled out loud, "Have you forgotten we are cut from the same cloth?"

Amy pulled up beside Lexia on her motorcycle.

Lexia turned quickly and hypnotized Amy with her demonic eyes.

"Battling with me is like battling with a hot torch. Don't touch me if you can't stand the heat!" warned Lexia.

Amy reverted to her conscious mind. "I don't want to touch you. I already know who you are and where you're from!" She reached into the top pocket of her jacket, pulled out a picture, and handed it to Lexia. "I thought you would love to have a picture of your mother." Amy cranked up her motorcycle and rode off, followed by two white cars.

Later that evening, Amy told her followers to go underground and give Alaysha a picture of her daughter that she had never seen. Little did Alaysha know that Amy had been the one following her all along!

Writing on the wall

From the strange homeless woman

Why weep now,

When we treat one another so badly!

CHAPTER 20

The time came for the biggest Presidential debate in history between Lexia and her twin brother, Luffa. The debate was held at Hofstra University in New York City. It was broadcast on every television network, including all local radio stations, cellphone apps, and even the new digital screen watches. People all over the world watched like children waiting for Santa Claus on Christmas Eve.

Sandra Goldman, a reporter from "Meet the Press," was present. She'd observed the two election candidates because they funded their own campaigns. The other candidates mysteriously dropped out. Goldman stood up energetically with a microphone in hand in front of a live camera and began to speak.

"Never before in Presidential history have two siblings, brother and sister, battled it out for the Oval Office in the White House!"

Then Tommy Brown, a reporter from "Fox News," stepped forward and began to speak live: "You said that right, Sandra. Never before in political history! Anyway, this is exactly what the country wanted—a woman to run for president once again, although we did elect a female vice president."

"There was a woman that ran for president in 1872, the second in 1972, and the third in 2016. And in the 2020 election, six women ran for president, the same in 2024. Now, today, women all over the United States truly believe this is the time for a woman to be Commander-in-Chief. Some say that before the 46th President stepped in, the 45th President ran America in a totally disastrous manner. He was actually impeached twice in one term, though not convicted in either of the subsequent trials. He tried to divide the American people; he even disrespected women, while a majority of his base constituents maintained that he was the best president the United States ever elected!" He was elected again in 2024.

"A few speculated that the 46th President tried his best; so did the 47th. There were so many comments, and many different opinions, but overall, the truth of the matter is the American people want a fair president, someone who doesn't lie to the general public to get elected and someone who will do what he promised to do."

"Americans want a president who will treat all American people the same— the rich, middle-class, even the poor—no matter what their ethnic background is. We are all the same. This is Tommy Brown reporting from 'Fox News'!"

Whitney Greene, a newscaster from CNN, was joined by Lawrence Adams, one of the newscasters from ABC, to announce the two presidential candidates as they both stepped onto the stage: "Democratic nominee, Lexia Taylor, and Republican nominee, Luffa Taylor."

The audience applauded for Lexia when she strode across the stage with an obvious "Switch" to her gait. She eventually reached her assigned post wearing a tight-fitting white leather suit.

Luffa wore a black cashmere suit, receiving generous applause from the crowd.

"Mr. Taylor, what is your definition of a woman being elected Commander-in-Chief?" asked Lawrence Adams.

Luffa walked slowly towards the crowd, catching the attention of every woman in the auditorium.

"I don't have anything against women," he spoke in a low tone. "I've always believed that women should have equal rights. But they should stay in their place. A woman is not equipped to run this country. There are many serious issues evolving around this country that need to be fixed. That is something only a man can do. Women are weak, soft creatures that should remain in the home on their backside, having babies and letting the man take full control as always!"

The women in the audience booed him.

"Don't let her menstrual cycle come on," he smiled. "We'll all be in trouble!"

There was laughter and heavy applause from the men. The crowd was asked politely to calm down.

"Ms. Taylor, do you believe in Mr. Taylor's statement about women?" asked Whitney Greene.

Lexia remained at her post and smiled back at her brother. "I do believe what you say, Luffa, is true!" She then turned and faced the audience, saying, "Yet those were the old days with old-time beliefs! It is a new era in a new age where women have grown stronger than men. We have the ability to do whatever a man can do and much better. I also truly believe a woman should be treated in a respectful fashion. We are women with children . . . Women that gave birth to men in this world that have grown up with hatred in their hearts to intimidate us with their sexual fantasies. I don't speak to crucify all men, just a few. If I'm elected president, I will see to it that there will be a high penalty for any man that disrespects any woman or engages in sexual assault!" Also, the constitutional law should not hold any rights over what a woman can do with her body while being pregnant.

The strange homeless woman entered through the auditorium doors. She pointed her finger at Lexia, and when she began to speak, tears of blood dripped from her eyes.

She said, "You speak with two tongues; frogs come leaping out of your mouth."

The security team quickly dragged the woman out of the auditorium. There was complete silence in the air. Then the audience applauded while Lexia and Luffa stared at each other. Lawrence Adams and Whitney Greene began asking political questions that needed to be addressed—from crime to unemployment, Medicare and Social Security, the minimum wage, child care, housing, education to nuclear missiles. Whitney Greene asked Luffa about taxes and foreigners. He said he wanted to lower taxes and keep foreigners from coming into the United States.

"Please!" Lexia interrupted bluntly. "The American people don't need another ignorant person."

The audience and photographers applauded with loud laughter. They were then asked to quiet down once again. The debate grew heated that night in New York, with multiple questions being asked. Even a few fights broke out when asked about gay rights.

"I don't believe in it!" Luffa replied.

"I disagree with you, Luffa," said Lexia, smiling devilishly. "It's time for everyone to come out of the closet so we all can play together!"

The crowd cheered once again in high spirits.

Then, finally, the debates were over.

And the votes were being counted!

Writing on the wall

From the strange homeless woman

Never let money be your God

For it, too, shall turn back to dust!

CHAPTER 21

At the age of one hundred and twelve, the Man of God was the oldest man living, and he still possessed the strength to maneuver swiftly on his own in his wheelchair. He received an emergency message to report to the Vatican at once! When the plane landed in Rome, the entire flight of passengers (except him) had died instantly. He rolled on his own in his wheelchair to the Vatican with no one to chauffeur him.

He witnessed such horrible activities. People and animals were dropping dead of an unknown disease in similar areas. Some people were down on their knees praying for death!

In a long line on each side of the plaza outside of the Vatican leading to the front entrance were priests and priestesses, archbishops, deacons, nuns, ministers, bishops, pastors and a few religious leaders who were speaking in an unknown tongue, bobbing their heads up and down with their eyes rolling back into their heads and white foam and blood bubbling out of their mouths.

He continued to roll his wheelchair right into the Pope's secret chamber.

The Pope sat alone, shivering to his bones.

"What is going on, Papa?" he asked slowly.

"I've held this secret for so many years," answered the Pope. "I didn't want the world to know the truth. This secret has been handed down from Pope to Pope for centuries! Sometimes words are better hidden in the dark, but all things must come to light! The world thought a man would rule over nations as the signs had shown for centuries."

"It started with the first woman, Eve. She ate the forbidden fruit first; man followed! In the story of Samson and Delilah, Samson promised God he would never tell of his strength from where it came. Samson told Delilah as he was weakened by her beauty!"

"The painting of Mona Lisa by Leonardo da Vinci in 1503 in Florence, Italy; the Statue of Liberty, a gift to the United States from France; a bronze statue of a woman; the freedom dome on top of the United States Capitol; the fearless girl statue facing the famous charging bull."

"AM Not is not a man. AM Not is a woman!"

A ghoul rose behind the Pope. Its long tongue moved swiftly out of its mouth like a raging snake touching the lips of the Man of God.

When the ghoul revealed itself, the Man of God panicked. When he saw it had been the kind woman he'd met years ago, he realized his appointed time of death was now! Blood dripped from the Pope's eyes as he sat paralyzed in his chair. The Man of God screamed in agony, holding his chest tightly. He gasped for air when the ghoul began to make demonic sounds that pierced his ears and whispered the words "I AM – I AM." Desperately and repeatedly he yelled: "AM Not . . . AM Not . . . AM Not." Sweat poured heavily down his face; in seconds, he had a massive heart attack and died!

The sun rose in Vatican City; the people that prayed for death met their fate that night. Multiple corpses lay in the blowing hot sand while the crows ate off their flesh!

And in the United States and all over the world, the people were appalled. Lexia Taylor became the first female President of the United States of America!

Writing on the wall

From the strange homeless woman

There is a God that sits high

And sees all that is done!

CHAPTER 22

O n the day of the inauguration, super-high-tech helicopters flew overhead in the cold blue skies.

Tears of happiness flooded the faces of 7.9 million people that waited patiently around the Washington, D.C. area and at the bottom of the U.S. Capitol steps, even around the entire world, to witness the 48th president be sworn in to occupy the White House! A woman named Susan Hill was sworn in first as vice president. At noon, Lexia flounced out in a tight red skirt and took the oath as the new Commander-in-Chief! In the background, the official Marine band began to play "Hail to the Chief," which was followed by a twenty-one-gun salute.

A little chaos erupted when a drunken, rowdy man yelled, "The beast is in control; may God have mercy on us all!"

Some crowd members kicked and stomped him. Security officials immediately dragged him away. Lexia laughed when she saw the delight of such bloody torture.

"Out with the old times; in with the new times," she yelled to the crowd. "You've read my post, signifying I'm taking America in a new direction. Remember, your 45th president stated, 'Let's Make America Great Again'! How can it be great when it was never great from the beginning? From slavery to poverty, people were being deprived of their homes. The cost of healthcare, food, and gas prices was outrageous! The shameless killing with guns on the streets is out of control. Corruption, crime, and unemployment are sky-high, and let us not forget about the homeless Americans!"

She paused for a moment. The crowd went hysterical. After they quieted down, Lexia continued her speech.

"America is a total mess, where our children don't get the education they deserve to grow up and work in a corporate world. Men and women who have fought for this country have no right to come home to nothing or beg for anything."

"There are countless cases of sexual assault on women. The predator sits back and laughs like he's done nothing wrong. Well, that's all about to change. We've paid the cost to be the boss. Women have rights, too!"

The crowd of women roared with excitement.

"We love you, Lexia!" was their cry.

A man stood next to his coworker, took a sip of beer from his cup, and angrily said, "Do you believe this shit?"

Lexia moved her hair from the right side of her eye. She noticed two women standing in the midst of the crowd, staring at her.

She smiled and continued once again, without the use of a teleprompter. She went on and addressed some serious issues concerning the economy.

Afterwards, the inauguration ball was held at the Walter E. Washington Convention Center. Laughter and excitement filled the atmosphere of the famous people. Even former presidents attended the celebration.

The lights went dim for a private moment, and Luffa was offered the first dance with his sister, as the band played instrumentals to "It's a Man's World" with the secondary refrain of "but it's nothing without a woman".

The two siblings collaborated back and forth in the middle of the floor, and the crowd stood aside and watched them closely.

"Dad is not happy," Luffa whispered closely into Lexia's ear.

"Who gives a damn? He's dried up!" she whispered back into his ear as she swirled in his arms.

"What about the last two presidents before you?"

"Please, Luffa." She leaned in towards him and replied, "They were just Daddy's pawns!"

"Oh really? What about you?" Luffa grinned.

"I'm the overseer of Hell!" Lexia laughed wildly.

Lexia quickly swirled into the arms of a soldier, leaving Luffa dancing by himself. At all four balls, Lexia took out time to dance with every soldier and every celebrity that attended. When the flashing lights stopped and the cameras went off, Lexia was able to relax her first night in the White House!

After she settled in as the Commander-in-Chief, she demolished every document the president before her had signed. With the help of her new democratic administration, she would do everything she promised the American people she would do. Lexia did things her way and didn't care about the Republican vote or what the House of Congress had to say.

Minimum wages rose to forty-five dollars an hour. Homes of people that lived in ghetto neighborhoods were transformed into middle-class homes.

Children received a better education with the promise of paid scholarships to college after graduation.

She ordered the criminal justice system to pardon prisoners who had been incarcerated for life.

"I believe every man and woman deserves a second and third chance in life for freedom!" she announced in one of her State of the Union speeches.

"Foreigners have a right to come into the United States to live in peace." She set out new rules and regulations for women's rights. She argued with every state governor and mayor that every homeless person should maintain a house of their own. Medicare health insurance was affordable; also affordable was gas for people who owned vehicles. CP5 robots were assigned to each household to do all the necessary cleaning and cooking, if needed.

One afternoon, Secretary of State Robert Rosenfeld texted Lexia some vital information that needed to be addressed. When he didn't receive a text message in return, he took it upon himself to personally go to the Oval Office. He knocked and waited patiently. A mysterious wind blew the door open. To his surprise, he witnessed the Commander-in-Chief and the Vice President making out in the nude on the Oval Office desk. Lexia removed her tongue from Susan's mouth.

"Besides running the country, this is what I also do best. You need to try me some time," she smiled, and she continued kissing Susan.

Robert Rosenfeld turned away, reaching for a handkerchief in his pocket. He wiped the sweat off his forehead and left the White House in a hurry to tell his wife what he had witnessed. A day later, Secretary of State Robert Rosenfeld and his wife were never heard from again!

Writing on the wall

From the strange homeless woman

Heaven holds no hate behind its gate

Only a glamorous light of love!

CHAPTER 23

Alaysha glimpsed at her daughter for the first time at the Presidential Inauguration. Seeing a photograph of her was not like seeing her in person. She couldn't believe how a woman as beautiful as her daughter existed!

She and Dorothy were the ones standing in the midst on that inauguration day.

Afterwards, they returned to the underground, although life on the surface had been good. The two knew it had been a great lie to deceive the people, and eventually Lexia's true colors would show . . . or maybe not.

She and Dorothy talked about the situation until they heard stories from various individuals who talked about the Lord.

One man mentioned he'd lived underground since the late 70's. He knew the wrath of God was coming soon in a world that Satan and his followers had so viciously taken over!

"God is still in control!" said an elderly woman. "It is us that went astray, doing wicked things to each other. The love has gone out of this world. We've forgotten to pray and have faith!"

"Stop talking rubbish, you old hag!" said someone in the crowd.

"I did everything right in my life. I went by the orders, followed the damn rules. My wife and two kids were shot to death inside a supermarket."

A voice then yelled out, "My brother was stabbed to death for five dollars, and he never messed with anybody!"

Everyone paused for a moment; then a crippled man came forward and spoke. "What I would like to know is if there is a God, why does he let bad things happen to us and make us suffer?"

The elderly woman put her hand on top of the cripple man's hand and stared around at everyone present.

"Stop blaming God for your mistakes. Everyone has free will of choice; some choices are good, others are bad, and some may lead to your early death. Generally speaking, God is not the blame; it is us!"

A man walked among the assembly with his wife and four children. "What's all the arguing about? We have a woman president. Me and my family are about to go back up in the world and live!"

Alaysha and Dorothy excused themselves from the provocative crowd and decided the same fate—to go back above the surface. The two had periodically gone through emotional trauma—Alaysha, with her daughter from Hell, and Dorothy with a son she never knew she'd given birth to.

Dorothy began to cry on Alaysha's shoulder as they walked through West Potomac Park, "I have a son out there somewhere. Even if he is a bad seed, I would love to see him!"

Alaysha gently stroked Dorothy's hair back. "You will eventually, Ms. Dorothy."

A week later, Dorothy ran into an old-time friend named Courtney. They'd met each other in the early eighties at Courtney's brother's wedding. He'd recently died of prostate cancer. Courtney worked in the Capitol Building as a state representative.

Since Dorothy and Alaysha didn't have shelter at the time, Courtney offered them her guest room. Late nights, they would drink red wine at the kitchen table and often converse about Courtney's job in the Capitol.

"Since that woman became president, it's been a lot of underhanded, mischievous things going on inside the White House."

"AM Not"

Feeling a little mellow after her third glass of wine, Alaysha twisted her lips sarcastically.

Courtney began to laugh as she took a sip of wine.

"If I told you what was going on, they would kill me!"

She laughed herself weary and went to bed.

When the sun rose the next morning, the house was quiet. Usually, Courtney would be up playing loud music while doing exercises.

"Courtney . . . Courtney!" Dorothy whispered and tiptoed out of the guest room, feeling light-headed. She'd heard running water from the faucet in the bathroom that guided her to walk in that direction. Feeling an evil presence, she opened the door slowly and almost fainted when she saw Courtney lying on the floor. She was incoherent with a two-headed black snake strangling her to death.

When she felt someone breathing heavily in her ear, she was too scared to turn around. She shut both eyes and ran quickly to the guest room to wake up Alaysha. Minutes later, they returned only to find a stiff corpse!

Writing on the wall

From the strange homeless woman

Some indulge in witchcraft at night

For fortune and fame

Being wealthy is all they care about!

CHAPTER 24

L uffa stopped twirling in circles in the governor's mansion. His eyes flinched, and then he tilted his head angrily when rumors began to circulate that Lexia had plans to run for another term.

Devising a plot to get rid of his sister, he left his mansion in California. He wanted to stop her from playing her own deceitful game.

Before she could begin her State of the Union address on gun control, one of Lexia's Secret Service men whispered in her ear that Luffa wanted to have a brief conversation with her in the public auditorium. However, she directed her men to have Luffa meet with her privately in the Oval Office. She entered the room with a disturbed appearance on her face.

"What is it, my one-time lost brother?"

Luffa's eyes squinted as Lexia walked to and sat down behind her desk.

"Give it up, Lexia; sit in the back seat!"

Lexia laughed like a little girl. "I will always be the driver, and you will always be the passenger," she retorted.

"I doubt that seriously." Luffa slammed his fist on the table, saying, "I have connections!"

Lexia leaned back in her chair and laughed again. "What connections, Luffa—these moronic souls?"

She reached into her desk drawer for a cigarette, lit it, and blew smoke rings in his face.

She stood up, fixed her skirt, and walked toward the door, opened it, and then turned and winked at him.

"Anyway, my one-time lost brother, I have to address the American people. Find your way out of my house before I have my men throw you out!"

Lexia addressed the American people, noting that firearms were about to be banned and, in their place, would be a new small device called Laser-Tech Six. With the push of a button, this device would release an invisible beam of light with a sting from which an individual would be rendered unconscious for fifteen minutes. In effect, this device would do no serious harm to the body. She touted that "In creating such a device, a suspect being apprehended would live to see another day without a hail of bullets being pumped into his body, leading to death. Furthermore, it would cut down gun violence." It was certain that some state officials and some of the American people were furious about this idea, not to mention gun store owners who would be put out of business!

A news reporter politely asked, "How am I supposed to protect my family when a so-called thug breaks into my house?"

There were no comments.

It had been only three years, and Lexia had become a threat to foreign countries. She had made certain trade deals and reneged on all of them. She later received a proposition from the Chinese government via text message.

She arrived in China hours later on Air Force One. She stepped off the plane with her Secret Service men and noticed five Chinese men waiting for her beside a white limousine.

Ordering her men to stay behind, she switched flirtatiously toward the men and was then chauffeured in by the driver, followed by the five Chinese men. As usual, she lit a cigarette and blew smoke rings in their faces.

"Well, China boys, have you come up with a proposition my ears would love to hear? Sorry to say that is my country's way," she smiled deviously.

The Chinese man seated next to her stared at her with an air of disgust, "You Americans forget we are the ones with the brains. Without us, your country would be worthless!"

"Maybe you have a point about those morons," said Lexia. "But your country is over the top with morons. That is why I'm taking America in a new direction, starting with your country first!"

"You crazy bitch, you can't do that," one of the Chinese men yelled.

Lexia's eyes turned dark red. She gripped him by his neck and started squeezing tightly as the other Chinese men watched in horror.

"Call me a bitch again, and I will destroy your whole generation in a second and demolish your entire country!"

She then released his neck and nimbly let herself out of the limo and boarded Air Force One on her way back to the United States of America, leaving the Chinese man gasping for air.

A mob of news reporters and paparazzi was standing in front of the White House when she stepped out of Cadillac One. She gave them a horrific stare that made them scared to approach her as she sauntered through the entrance gate.

Suddenly, gunshots fired at her missed her head by an inch. The Secret Service men covered her quickly and moved her inside the White House.

In seconds, the person that fired the gun was shot to death by White House snipers perched on its roof. A few hours later, she held a meeting in the West Wing with her Secret Service men and military personnel, including the Secretary of State.

"I specifically indicated the other day that all firearms were to be banned, but apparently these morons are still in possession of this deadly tool." She paused for a moment.

"I want all guns removed from every household in this country—immediately!"

The Secretary of State flinched, "Madame President, we don't have the right to invade people's privacy."

Lexia walked over to him and yelled in his ear, "Don't tell me about rights. I have the right to do anything I damn please!"

That night, all around the United States, millions of people's homes and vehicles on highways were invaded by the Elite Special Forces. Anyone found with a firearm was thrown in jail for 90 days, even if the person was found with a license to carry.

With all the commotion going on, Alaysha and Dorothy had gone back underground with the mole people until the Elite Special Forces came and invaded them, too.

A few people ran for their lives while others stayed behind and were shot to death.

Alaysha flagged down an oncoming vehicle to drive her and Dorothy to the Washington National Cathedral. Inside, candles were lit, and people were on their knees praying.

When the wreckage calmed down on the outside, the doors opened wide. A short, bald-headed man dressed in a long white robe and glowing like an angel from Heaven entered with a five-year-old child named Deja by his side. The man held up in his right hand a medium-sized golden crucifix or cross, at which he exclaimed, "Unclean spirits, leave this place now!"

Without hesitation, a few people stood up and ran out of the cathedral! The man slowly looked around, staring at those who stayed behind.

"I'm searching for a woman named Alaysha Falls!"

Alaysha looked surprised when she heard the man call her name. She walked over and extended her arm toward him.

"I'm Alaysha Falls. Why are you looking for me?"

The man placed the cross in his side pocket and extended his hand as well. "It is a pleasure to meet you. My name is Cartesian. I am the successor to the Man of God."

Dorothy quickly walked over and bowed her head.

"My name is Dorothy Brooks. I've often wondered what happened to the Man of God."

After the man introduced Deja, he told them the story of what happened to the Man of God. When he finished, chills ran through Dorothy's bones.

Out of curiosity, Alaysha asked the question: "How did something so sinister walk on sacred ground?"

Cartesian inhaled deeply; then he exhaled slowly with his head bowed in shame. "Little boys were being molested by ordained ministers they greatly respected. A few religious leaders withheld vital information from the public. The holy grounds were cursed, which allowed evil to enter."

Deja walked forward and placed seven miniature gold crosses in Alaysha's hand and smiled.

Alaysha kneeled down and looked the little girl in her eyes. "What am I supposed to do with these crosses?" she asked.

"She cannot speak or hear," said Cartesian. "Neither can the rest of the children."

The cathedral doors opened slowly. Three little boys and three little girls entered.

Dorothy grinned to herself, recalling a well-known biblical passage: "And children shall lead the way!"

Writing on the wall

From the strange homeless woman

Some think they know of this World.

In reality, they know nothing.

Fore we all are dirt waiting to return

To the soil of the earth!

CHAPTER 25

The presidential election had passed, and once again, Lexia won the presidency. The Republicans were in total disbelief and highly upset at Lexia's victory. Foreign leaders were in dismay and were ready to start a war with the United States after she had declared all firearms be demolished at once and after she had taken power and control over one hundred and ninety-five other countries.

Although the spread of COVID-19 and its delta and omicron variant viruses had slowed down, we were on high alert for other new and deadly viruses.

After months in office, the news went viral on social media when Lexia traveled to England and seduced the prince and then bluntly told the queen to "Step down from her throne!"

It was reported later when Lexia returned that she had held a late-night orgy with her entire staff on the White House lawn. Republicans, state senators, governors, mayors, city councilmen, and community activists who were not affiliated with her organization signed a petition to have her immediately impeached.

"She is running the White House like a vigilante," a republican posted on social media.

Many Americans felt differently about the situation. They praised Lexia for her work ethic, even though she'd banned guns after someone aimed and shot at her head.

If the bullet had made contact with her brain, she would have been the fifth president to have been assassinated after Abraham Lincoln, James A. Garfield, William McKinley, and John F. Kennedy.

Meanwhile, in New York City, an elderly couple had just finished their afternoon grocery shopping. After the cashier totaled the bill, the man handed over six twenty-dollar bills.

"Sorry, sir, we no longer accept cash," announced the cashier.

The elderly man placed the loose bills back into his wallet and removed a debit card.

"Sorry, sir, we no longer accept those either!"

"So, what do you accept?" asked the man angrily.

The cashier directed them to an electronic machine in the corner of the store. "You have to download all your information on the site's computer, even your religion. Then, a YL digital currency card will be mailed to you in three to five business days. At that time, you can purchase your items as if the Real ID card were not enough.!"

When the woman made an obscene remark, the security guard removed the elderly couple from the store. They went to another store run by man-made robots and were told the same thing.

That same day, Luffa stormed onto the White House property with his bodyguards. They were told by Lexia's Secret Service men to wait on the outside until they received word from the Commander-in-Chief.

"Do you believe this—I have to have permission to see my own sister!"

Within seconds, they were allowed in to meet with Lexia in the Oval Office.

"I dare you, Lexia," yelled Luffa, coming through the door. "You're trying to take my position from underneath me!"

Lexia flashed a devilish grin. "You have no position!"

Luffa charged towards her, but he was stopped in his tracks by her Secret Service men. He shook his finger at her in rage. "Have you forgotten who is really running the show?"

Lexia spun around in her chair and lit a cigarette. "If you are talking about Daddy, his ace of spades is out the window!"

Holding the top of his head, Luffa twirled. He began stomping up and down on the floor like a child in a temper tantrum. "Have you lost your mind? You can't override Dad!"

Apparently, in a state of distress, the Secretary of State entered the Oval Office. "Madam President, you cannot declare war on any of these foreign countries! The United States Constitution grants only Congress that sole power!" He politely placed some papers on the office table before her eyes! The countries listed were Japan, China, North Korea, Jerusalem (Israel), and Russia.

Lexia got up from her chair and slammed it down behind her as she walked towards her brother and the Secretary of State.

"Have you two morons forgotten that I'm the most powerful bitch in the world? I can do anything I damn please!"

This time, Luffa pushed Lexia's Secret Service men to the side and went face-to-face with his sister.

"You've gone beyond Hell. You want to play bang, bang, shoot 'em up— you've got it, sister! Now watch my smoke!"

Lexia laughed as Luffa stormed out. "Whatever! See you in Hell, Luffa!"

The Secretary of State whispered in the ear of one of Luffa's bodyguards as he followed behind them, "Either she is going through menopause or her menstrual cycle is on!"

Writing on the wall

From the strange homeless woman

People of the World of all colors

Confess your sins to the Creator of this World

So in the end of time

Your name will be written in the Book of Life!

CHAPTER 26

S trange and unusual events were beginning to happen in every state. Governors, mayors, news reporters, and even authors who had written books against the president had mysteriously vanished without a trace!

The entire Federal Bureau of Investigation team had even disappeared and was replaced with Lexia's followers.

Police brutality became the norm. Racism still affected some people in certain cities, while Mother Nature released her fury with tornadoes and terrifying rain storms that caused bridges to collapse and even planes and flying cars to fall from the sky.

Alaysha felt her blood boil deep within when she heard these eerie things going on in the world. Her thoughts still haunted her, reminding her of the messenger's words.

"What has become of us?" she sniffled next to Deja.

Dorothy gently placed her hand on Alaysha's shoulder.

"We are all Devil worshippers. Periodically, we lie, steal, kill, and even commit adultery; everything God told us not to do—we do the opposite, not realizing the consequences!"

"We are not worshippers of Satan."

Cartesian smiled for a brief moment. "It is the person's mindset that makes him believe such a thing is true!"

The three of them and the seven children were peacefully living in a little townhouse outside of Washington—away from the wreckage of the world. As the nights turned into days, their food supplies began to dwindle.

Cartesian, at one time, knew of a couple of churches where he could get food if a crisis were to happen, such as this one. But since Lexia's second term in office, all church doors were closed to the public. She could not stand the sight of a church, nor even to walk on holy property. Neither one of them possessed a YL currency card.

Alaysha made up her mind to drive Cartesian's car into the disastrous city to see if she could get some help.

Dorothy wanted to go for the ride, but her mind and body would not let her go, and she was at the age where she could hardly walk.

Before Alaysha left, she squeezed Dorothy tightly in her arms with tears falling from her eyes. It would be a long ride, and who knows if she would make it back alive.

"I want to thank you for being here with me!"

Dorothy laughed a little and began to stroke Alaysha's hair back and forth.

"I'm just going to sit here and ask the Lord for forgiveness. I am scared of Hell; I don't want to be tortured in Satan's mischievous fire!"

Alaysha hugged the children before she left. While driving, she remembered that she had asked Cartesian how she would recognize a demon.

He said to her warmly, "Judge the characteristics of the individual."

She drove a distance until a Washington police officer directed her to take another route.

"What's the problem?" she yelled at the officer while rolling down the window.

"A pedophile was luring children into the alleyway up the street," said the officer.

"Were any of the children hurt?" she asked out of concern.

"I can't answer that question, Ma'am."

Hoping no one had noticed her making a U-turn, she drove halfway down the block and parked. She walked quickly back up the street and snuck past the officers when she saw photographers in the alleyway.

There were brief messages written on a wall.

In the corner against the wall sat the same naked, homeless woman in handcuffs that Alaysha had seen when she was a teenager. Alaysha bit her lip until it bled as the woman raised her head slowly and stared deeply into her eyes.

The woman said in a slow, dry voice, "You were the one that birthed the whore bastard into this world. Within a year's time if this whore is not stopped, this Earth will be no more!"

The homeless woman hypnotized Alaysha for a period of time. A vision appeared of a man dressed in a long white robe sexually abusing young girls and boys in the dark. It appeared as many unknown faces that she could not clearly recognize.

"What the hell!" one of the officers yelled.

Her disturbing vision came to an instant end.

The homeless woman vanished into a pile of dust. Alaysha ran out of the alleyway back up the block to where she had parked the car, and she sped off down the road.

Writing on the wall
From the strange homeless woman

For the children of the world today
It does not pay to be a bully
For there will come a time

When someone will intimidate you
And you will fear for your life!

CHAPTER 27

Since Canada was top number one country in the world, Lexia announced to Canada's prime minister that he should resign from his position.

When he ignored her command, she promised there would be war with his country, just as she had promised the other foreign countries.

The United Nations sent for her after signing a new law that everyone around the world should possess YL (your life) digital currency cards implanted with a special microchip to spy on an individual's daily activities since the flat screens, smart phones, and other new digital devices didn't offer much progress in capturing data.

"You cannot control the world, Madame President," said the UN's chief administrative officer.

Lexia lit a cigarette and ordered them all to go to Hell!

Luffa, exasperated with his sister's jezebel spirit, returned to Russia. He'd been friends with the Russian President since Lexia wanted to control Russia.

She found it hilarious to learn that Russia had a nuclear missile called Satan 2. She reclaimed the American people's hopes and dreams that she had once given them. Only the ones that did not follow her commands and her wishes would she demand and claim their souls!

When the Lincoln Memorial had been removed and a statue of herself put into its place, the news once again went viral on social media. Even the etching "In God We Trust" was taken down in every courtroom around the United States and replaced with "In Lexia We Trust!" As time went on and her demands were not met by other countries, she began to meditate secretly alone at night in the Oval Office, conjuring up Abraxas, Abyzou, Amy, Anyact, and Lahash—evil spirits from Hell!

At the same time, Cartesian called on the seven archangels—Michael, Gabriel, Raphael, Uriel, Sealtiel, Jehudiel, and Barachiel. After he'd witnessed a corpse at a funeral sitting up in a coffin on fire, screaming and yelling in agony, "Please God, have mercy on me," the biggest war since the beginning of time in the spiritual realm between good and evil had begun.

Cartesian and Dorothy were worried about Alaysha's whereabouts. It had been a week since she had left to find food. The seven children huddled in a circle. Dorothy and Cartesian fasted. Although they both were dispirited, they never gave up their faith in God.

Suddenly, they heard footsteps outside. When the door cracked open slowly, Alaysha walked in with a few prayer warriors. Each one of them carried a bag of food and bottles of spring water to quench their thirst.

Surprised at seeing Alaysha, Dorothy said, "Thank God, you returned safely!" The children came out of their huddles and joined the prayer warriors as they sat comfortably and ate the fresh food. Alaysha told them about the strange homeless woman and the writing on the wall.

She even mentioned seven glowing stars from the East that led her to an abandoned church where she met the prayer warriors.

"It was the seven archangels," said Cartesian.

Seeing everyone content, he told them to remain calm and lie low until he returned from visiting the new Pope at the Vatican. Dorothy became extremely concerned.

"How will you make it past the Elite Special Forces without a YL ID card?"

Cartesian turned towards Dorothy and flashed a little smile.

"I fear no man; God will protect me as always!"

At Washington Dulles International Airport, passengers glanced at him strangely as he walked past security and onto a flight heading to Italy without a YL identification card. The Vatican appeared deserted when he arrived, except for the same weird scenery that appeared before his eyes that his successor before him had also witnessed. A line of religious leaders, with their eyes rolling back in their heads and white foam coming out of their mouths, meandered up to the entrance of the Vatican.

When the Pope could not be found on the Vatican premises, it startled him. Cartesian quickly returned to the United States to warn his friends that something sinister was happening. He found only a small amount of powdery residue on the ground left over from the small house where he had left his friends.

Writing on the wall

From the strange homeless woman

When you have nothing left to fight

With and all hope is gone,

Fight with the Word of God!

CHAPTER 28

The United States was about to undergo a thermo-nuclear war attack from China and North Korea after Lexia had refused negotiations she'd promised on certain trade deals!

She sent for more demons to go out into the world to do evil to those that would not abide by her new laws.

Luffa could sit back no longer and watch his sister step into the shoes that should have been his. To signify his taking charge, he immediately took over the Russian Presidency after his followers invaded the country.

In a meeting, he warned her to resign her position as the President of the United States, and if she failed to listen, he would detonate a Satan 2 ballistic nuclear missile.

Lexia laughed hysterically. "I don't give a damn what you do! Just know that you're going to Hell first, and I will still be in charge there, too."

Meanwhile, Cartesian wandered around the area looking for his missing friends. He was devastated when a gray cat with dark yellow eyes appeared in front of him. The animal made terrible noises. So did the man that followed. Blood dripped from the man's nose and out of his ears; then his skin began to melt like butter in a hot cast-iron frying pan. Cartesian pulled a hanging branch off a leaning tree, dangled it in front of the man's face, and yelled out loud: "Get thee behind me, demons from Hell!" Within minutes, the man and cat burst into flames and scattered into the ground beneath him.

Cartesian then heard a woman crying behind some tall bushes, not too far from where he was standing. When he forced the leaning tree to the side, he cautiously watched Alaysha, down on her knees, weeping in sorrow with the seven children and prayer warriors who were also saddened. Not too far under the old, withered tree, a body lay motionless, concealed under brown leaves. And above, spiritual angels prepared the soul of the body to rest.

Cartesian came to the realization that they were shedding tears over Dorothy's death. He gently lifted Alaysha by her hand and held her in his arms.

"She is at peace with the Lord," he whispered in her ear, and then he led Alaysha away from the others so that they could talk in private.

"These will be the last and final days if we don't stop the president."

Alaysha stared at him in curiosity. "Why do we have to talk alone?"

Cartesian smirked a little. "It's not for everyone to hear the words I speak!" He handed her a folder from the side pocket of his robe.

"What is this about?" she asked while opening the folder.

"I've confiscated it from the Vatican. A few of the archbishops, pastors, ministers, and deacons serve the Madam President," Cartesian replied.

Alaysha began scratching her head. "What about the Pope?"

Cartesian went into deep thought for a moment. "The Pope must be in hiding, praying with the cardinals unless he is a follower, too!"

Suddenly, several high-tech military helicopters flew above and surrounded the area. Military troops climbed down on a variety of swinging ropes and ushered them to a secret data bank outside of Washington. Later, they returned to retrieve the children and the prayer warriors.

When inside, Alaysha was surprised to see people from the Federal Bureau of Investigation present among them. So were members from the Central Intelligence Agency, the United States Marine Corps, and the Department of Homeland Security. She was most shocked to see Amy.

Amy squeezed Alaysha tightly in her arms and kissed her on the lips. "I'm glad you've made it here safely."

Alaysha pretended not to be astonished after the kiss. She gently pushed away and proceeded to look around like a little lost child. Cartesian and the others were taken to another section while Amy freely continued showing Alaysha around the data bank. "This place is amazing. I can't believe how far technology has advanced through the years."

Amy sat on a table near her and chuckled, "It truly is amazing. This place has been here for many decades, waiting for a day such as this one!"

With her head down, Alaysha frowned, "We started this as teenagers, not to mention my grandmother engaged in witchcraft!"

Cartesian walked into the room and interrupted them, "The world started this madness with greed, jealousy, and hatred for one another. The world gave birth to these evil Twins!!"

Alaysha leaned against the wall, nodded her head, and began to gasp for air. Tears drifted from her eyes as she asked, "Why did it have to come from me?"

"Sometimes God works in mysterious ways, and so does the Devil," said Cartesian.

He continued his earlier conversation with Alaysha, this time with Amy present. He told them there had always been scandals in the Vatican. Certain books had been removed from the Bible, and it is forbidden for anyone to read them.

Amy tilted her face upwards, asking, "Where are these books now?"

"These books are closely guarded in the Vatican archives," answered Cartesian.

He went on to mention that the Vatican had 1,400 rooms and went under construction on April 18, 1506. On the other hand, the White House had 132 rooms and went under construction on October 13, 1792. "These two buildings have many deep secrets," he exclaimed.

Military trucks were heard driving up on the premises. The alarms went off. When the automatic security doors opened, Sergeant Hanover and his U.S. Army troops entered with their M101 semi-automatic, long-range sniper rifles and other powerful machine guns.

He had once worked with Lexia until she replaced him with one of her followers. Everyone in the data bank ran front and center when they heard the commotion and the sergeant.

"We have to shut the White House down immediately and get that psychopathic woman out of there now!"

The satellite computer board suddenly flashed an electrical disturbance that showed newscaster Lawrence Adams and a few people standing beside him shivering with unimaginable fear on their faces. Adams began to speak slowly into the microphone:

"This is Lawrence Adams from ABC Live! We've just received word that Russia, China, and North Korea are planning to launch their nuclear missiles at the dawn of October 13, 2035, toward the United States of America if our Madam President continues with her threats and tactics of stupidity, which claim her control over the world. If this happens, it will be the end of human civilization!"

There was another electrical disturbance—demonic goats rampaged through the streets of Washington, attacking innocent civilians. Alaysha started to panic wildly. "The thirteenth is two days away!"

More fleets of military trucks drove onto the premises with additional troops and the captain, this time with dozens of tanks following behind them. Everyone saluted the captain when he entered the data bank. He saluted back and stood firmly, saying: "We have a serious problem!"

Sergeant Hanover spoke briefly, "Like I mentioned earlier, we get that psychopathic woman out of the White House and reconcile with these foreign countries."

Amy stared up at the ceiling. "We can't just bombard the White House like those crazy fools did at the Capitol seventeen years ago!"

Cartesian came forward and asked the captain if he could have a private moment with Alaysha and Amy.

"We are about to go up against an evil force more powerful than any one of us. I pray we make it out alive!"

"There are millions of people here and even in foreign countries," said Alaysha, "Who are hungry and cold, with nowhere to go and with their children. Some are being killed for their belief in Jesus. We can't sit back and let this continue!"

Cartesian agreed, and so did Amy. Before they could interact with everyone on the data bank, Cartesian reminded them that no one at the data bank knew Amy and Alaysha were the mothers of these twin demons! They wondered whether the captain had a strategy to get rid of both Lexia and Luffa.

While words were being exchanged, Deja and the other six children formed a circle while holding hands. The lights went out, and the White House appeared in a blurred vision and then disappeared. When the lights came back on, the troops were amazed, and so were the captain and the sergeant.

Cartesian explained about the seven children and what they were about to go up against.

The sergeant nodded his head up and down. "We always thought it would be an alien or AI attack, not a demon attack!"

"It's time to Pray and Believe," said Cartesian.

Writing on the wall

From the strange homeless woman

Prayer is powerful if you believe

Let no one tell you anything different

For there is only one God

And he is the great and mighty I AM!

NEW CHAPTER 29

Amy pressed down on the alarm signal to get everyone prepared for a battle. She hurried to the basement with her crew. They retrieved a Heckler and Koch and ump's FN F2000 assault rifles, M60's and Mark 38's. She held Alaysha's arms tightly and kissed her gently on her lips before boarding a private jet with the captain heading to Russia.

The sergeant went with his troops in their military trucks and tanks up Pennsylvania Avenue towards the White House with a crowd of people following along, singing "Satan, we're going to tear your kingdom down."

Alaysha, Cartesian, and the seven children followed the prayer warriors on a transit metro bus to gather other believers. She finally put the pieces together of what the seven children were demonstrating. It was time for everyone to put their religious beliefs aside and come as one and pray the demon and her followers out of the government!

Although social media could not reach people entirely, people in the lower-class areas found a way to come together and pray through the madness. A few rich and wealthy people stayed hidden in their underground bunkers.

Through these crucial times around the world, strange and unusual things began to happen. The dead that were not of Christ rose from their fiery graves and rampaged through the streets yelling, "Please, Lord, forgive me!" Stores were damaged and set on fire; little children were being trampled upon as they tried to get out of the way of the chaos that plagued the streets. Animals broke out of city zoos and went berserk. Oceans near every state, even in foreign countries, turned into blood; then into a blaze of fire. Buildings and bridges came tumbling down. Even flying cars fell from the skies, not to mention a disturbing malfunction in the super AI robots. In Italy, the Vatican was surrounded by tourists and angry residents demanding the release of the books that were stripped from the Bible. China, North Korea, and Japan were exercising their rights and preparing for war, while citizens of the United States thought it was a war for control. Little did they know it subsisted in an evil spiritual warfare for power.

Cartesian and Alaysha were quickly led into a military tank facing the White House. The tank commander advised them to wear tanker helmets. Alaysha held on tightly to a side-bar and in an instant, she remembered Amy had inserted an Apple digital screen watch in her front pants pocket and displayed the digital watch in her hand. She pressed different numbers until a video flashed on and caught her immediate attention. Then she observed a strange bash in the U.S. Capitol building with top-name celebrities and people in official high offices. Money, sex, and recreational drugs were present. Fentanyl, X 10, ecstasy 666, perks 5,000, codeine triple X, along with marijuana, PCP, and cocaine. The video clip showed the Madam President swinging provocatively, half-naked, around a stripper pole in Las Vegas. The next video showed Luffa trying to make a peace offering with his sister to step down from the presidency so that he could take control of the office. After Lexia had consumed a strong alcoholic beverage, she sat next to him and rudely told him:

"It will never happen, my Brother from Another Mother. You and Daddy will always be beneath me. You are nothing but a piece of shit beneath my feet!"

Luffa stood up from his chair like a demented person and threw his empty glass to the floor. The shattering noise made the disc jockey stop the music, and the crowd quietened.

"I'm a piece of shit? You are the piece of shit trying to take over dad's kingdom. When I get to Russia, I am going to send that ballistic missile so far up your ass that you're going to be begging Dad and his legions to pull it out!"

Lexia grinned at Luffa.

"Stop being Daddy's bitch!"

She faced the crowd and held her glass high.

"Tonight, I will not dictate man-made laws. I am the law:
When I eat, you eat.
If I don't eat, you will not eat
I am your successor and your oppressor. I am your
Commander-in-Chief and from this night on, I am your god!"

These words mysteriously echoed in Alaysha's ear. Everyone that attended the party kneeled down to her and praised her as if she was a god!

When she snatched her skirt off and revealed herself boldly, Alaysha noticed that she had birthed a hermaphrodite!

She came across a video that saddened her heart to watch the midget-ville community attacked and removed from their homes and placed into a concentration camp with other Americans to await their mass execution on the premise that they did not worship her as their god. Even the Native Americans lost their reservations under her executive orders.

Not wanting her to see his tears, Cartesian leaned sideways, turning away from Alaysha, sniffling and catching his breath at the same time. Alaysha noticed his silent treatment and asked him kindly, "What is the problem?" Appearing depressed, he immediately turned facing her with watery eyes.

"When I was a child, my parents taught me to fear only the Lord. Now, for some apparent reason, I'm dreading having to face this demon!" The feeling of displeasure overwhelmed Alaysha's mind on hearing these words from a holy man.

"Tell me, Cartesian, was it fear that killed the man of god!"

Cartesian squeezed the tears from his eyes with his fingers, holding his head down in distress.

"What we fear the most usually comes for us at the end!"

Alaysha inhaled deeply and breathed out slowly. Then she whispered:

"That thing I birthed into the world, her first four years in office, she drastically changed America for the good. She accomplished elements no President had ever conquered in history!"

Cartesian smirked a little:

"She didn't have to answer to anyone. She made her own rules!" After a minute of silence, the tank commander tried to communicate with the lieutenant, but the reception kept experiencing interference.

A few Secret Service individuals were employed in Lexia's administration in different foreign countries under her command. Even the one hundred and fifty-five crew that occupied the International Space Station were under supervision, except China's Tiangong Space Station.

A private leak from an American news reporter stationed in North Korea stated the supreme leader has ordered his troops to expand for war with the United States within seven hours if Madam President does not reconcile with their government's terms and policies. He is also planning to launch the nuclear-armed Intercontinental Ballistic Missile H wasung-17, which could reach the U.S. in thirty-three minutes!

Cartesian removed his helmet from his head and declared: "It is time I face this demon alone!" As he exited slowly, Cartesian advised Alaysha to wait inside the tank until further instructions from the tank commander.

The soldiers quickly stood to attention and raised their firearms towards the White House. When four of Lexia's Secret Service men appeared to accompany Cartesian down the pathway, he turned towards the soldiers, asking them politely to lower their weapons. "This is not man's war; this is a spiritual warfare between good and evil!"

The soldiers lowered their firearms as they continued to walk up the pathway, followed by miniature drones inside what used to be the White House, now a deserted place occupied by demons.

The four men accompanied him to the diplomatic reception room on the south side, where Lexia stood in the middle of the floor with her back turned, making eerie, demonic sounds. The men left the two alone, closing the door tightly behind them. When she turned to face Cartesian, he resided in a paralyzed state and was attracted to her beauty. He watched nervously as her tongue slid viciously out of her mouth like a writhing snake, touching his lips gently, then slowly moving back into her mouth. She walked closer to him, revealing her breasts, transforming his mind away from his godly faith. She whispered softly in his ear, "I want to feel you inside me!"

Cartesian lingered under her demonic spell, which was pulling her closer to him. Making eye contact, stroking her hair backwards, he instantly sprang free from her spell. He pushed away and yelled:

"The words off your tongue are filthy. It shall rot and you shall speak no more."

Lexia clutched his hand and swirled herself against him, laughing loudly. "You are definitely not a true man of your god. Your eyes speak to me; you desire to have my body!"

Four miniature camera drones instantly zoomed in on Cartesian, removing his clothing quickly and laying her down on the couch. Turning her over, he tore off her skirt and began to deeply penetrate her from behind. She moaned and then laughed, "You so-called man of your god!"

He immediately pushed himself up off her when he noticed blood dripping out of his eyes onto the couch. Standing buck naked in the middle of the floor, crying hysterically, he began to speak nervously in a high-toned voice as that of a child about to get a spanking for being bad. He bent down, reaching for his pants, and removed a small bible from his front pocket, placing it on the floor in front of him.

"My Father, what I have done before you is an abomination. I have no right to enter the Kingdom of Heaven. Those who do wickedness in the dark will come to light. Those that lie, cheat, and steal. Those that commit sexual immorality, kill for no purpose, and use the Lord's name in vain will not enter the Kingdom of Heaven . . . if they do not repent and believe!"

White foam began to bubble out of his mouth. When his eyes rolled back, turning a dark red color, he ran towards the window, leaping through the glass. Shattered pieces followed him as he ran down towards the soldiers, buck-naked, also yelling the words repeatedly as the man of God did before him. AM NOT . . . AM NOT . . . AM NOT…

The lieutenant ordered his soldiers to attention and to raise their firearms as they discharged multiple bullets at him. Inside the tank, Alaysha's eyes widened. She covered her mouth after witnessing Cartesian fall dead to the ground.

Suddenly, eight black vans were seen far off on miniature camera drones driving viciously and honking their horns through the crowd of people on the streets of Washington. When the vans came to a halt in front of the White House, a woman departed from the first vehicle with five AI robots carrying automatic rifles in their hands. The lieutenant tilted his head to the side, "Excuse me, who the hell are you?"

The woman flung her hair from her eyes. "My name is Jack Ward, captain of the special AI elite force. We are here to take this lunatic Madam President out of position."

The lieutenant half-smiled. "If it were that easy, Captain, don't you think we would have handled the situation?"

Jack Ward dismissively stared at the soldiers. "I don't believe so; you and your men do not have the right artillery or ammunition!"

"Nowadays, you women think you know more than men," chuckled the lieutenant.

She faced her head down to the ground and breathed in deeply:

"Maybe we do know more than men. I am not here to argue with you. All I know is there are twenty-two foreign countries at war with each other, not to mention the United States is involved, and we are at war with each other because of this president!"

Before the lieutenant could say another word, a mysterious voice spoke out among them. "The battle is not for us to fight. It is Yeshua's battle."

"It is time we put our religion aside. Whether you are a Catholic, Jehovah's Witness, Muslim, Seventh-Day Adventist, Israelite, Buddhist—whatever your belief, put it aside. We all must come together as one and pray for peace so that Yeshua can heal the land. We cannot go up against such a force so evil and more powerful than us. The only way is to pray and believe!"

The mysterious voice came from the Pope. He came out of his secret chamber. Protected by Michael, the most powerful Archangel, he managed his way through the chaos outside the Vatican unseen. Few religious leaders connected with him, and a million people to pray not only around the White House but throughout the entire world.

Alaysha appeared in front of the Pope, hugging him with full respect. He began rubbing Holy Chrism on the top of her head.

"You must go in alone, my Child, and face your demon. May Yahweh have mercy on your soul!" he gently whispered in her ear.

When Alaysha stepped foot in the front door of the White House, the scenery occurred dark and gloomy. Blood dripped from the eyes of the dead presidents' portraits hanging on the wall along the hallway. As she walked closer towards the Oval Office, a demonic scream frightened her soul with a cold chill!

While turning the door knob slowly and opening the door her eyes widened with fear when she witnessed an Archbishop kneeling down to kiss the hand of the Madam President. When he turned facing towards her, his eyes were dark red and his tongue slivered out of his mouth like a snake; he hissed at her with deadly intent. The room was overwhelmed with pastors, preachers, religious leaders, celebrities, one former President, two former Vice Presidents, with the gaze of evil on their faces!

Meanwhile, dawn had come, and the moon rose over the White House. China, North Korea, and Israel had launched their nuclear missiles toward the United States of America.

When the Captain and Amy arrived in Moscow, flying over the 1st building where Luffa resided, missiles were fired at their jet. The captain fired back, only to make Luffa launch the ballistic nuclear missile Satan 2 also towards the United States.

His eyes turned a burning red in color.

"Damn you, Lexis!" he screamed horrifically as the jet crashed into the building. The ground opened up and swallowed him and his men in a blaze of fire!

Back in America, each window of the White House shattered into an explosion of flames when Lexis heard the crowd of people outside. They were holding hands and praying around the White House. She commanded the Secretary of State to launch all the ballistic missiles.

"It is Finished, Mother," Lexia spoke in a deep, demonic voice. "The world followed my Father since the beginning of time with their lust, greed, lies, and hate. Some even sold their precious souls for wealth and fame! Now they follow me, the god that was torn from the pages of history. I am the ruler of this world."

"You're not the Ruler of this world," yelled Alaysha.

"I pray that every demonic person in this room burns in the lake of fire for eternity!"

Lexia laughed. "You imbecile, get real. Are you serious? I am the one that fixed a Broken Deficit, gave a higher raise on Social Security, and good-paying jobs. I made the American people believe in themselves again. Now they have the freedom to do whatever they want. It's been something they always wanted to do all along. I am the savior of this World. I am the Mighty I AM!"

Suddenly, a strong wind blew into the room. Deja had never heard a voice in her young life, but such words coming from a satanic person restored her hearing. She entered the room and held up the Seven Gold Crosses and spoke loudly and clearly . . . "AM NOT!"

The White House began to shake as the prayers on the outside were prayers for peace. Every nuclear missile that flew in the open sky mysteriously exploded in mid-air and then vanished, resulting in a strong, concussive effect.

Lexia's face peeled and her eyes, too, turned a burning red color when she noticed the floor beneath her opened wide and a huge two-headed snake came up from the pits of hell and pulled her and the Archbishop, and everyone in the room except Alysha and Deja down within the flames.

Lexia's words echoed in the air: "My Father in Hell, Why have you forsaken me?"

Alaysha screamed as fire rose up her body. Tears poured down her face with abandon. Then a beam of light from the sky flashed on her through the White House window. The burning flames disappeared from her body. She smiled when she saw her mother and Dorothy's spirits, and the seven archangels.

Then there was a loud, deep voice from the sky.

"YAHWEH, JEHOVAH, I AM, I AM."

The entire Earth shook, and those that were not of Yeshua (Jesus) burned to ashes. Even the demons that had scaled the walls of the Capitol building burst into ashes.

The sun shone brightly, and the Pope appeared in the mist, and the Archbishop was Dorothy's lost son that she had never met—Tillman.

The next President of the United States of America is

_____?

THE BEGINNING

I t was said that it happened in the ancient days. The actual time or year was not recorded; nevertheless, it was never to be told!

A troublesome elderly king by the name of Victor and his fleet of men came trampling on their horses into a deserted village in Rome searching for a mysterious woman that was believed to have given birth to Satan's twins.

According to the legend, this woman had been kidnapped. Prophets believed this woman had been brutalized and molested by Satan himself!

"Bring all the pregnant women to me naked," yelled King Victor. "If you men capture such a woman that has the mark of the beast on her left thigh, she is the one that withholds the bastard twins!"

Rachel was her name, a destitute brunette with hazel eyes and a pale-dry face. She even walked with a limp in her left leg. She stepped forward and kneeled before the King and admitted it was she that withheld the unwanted twins.

A disturbed appearance showed on the King's face as he glanced down at the woman. "Remove your garments at once," he commanded.

When removing her garments, he pointed his sword down between her legs and then, without hesitation, he slapped the woman backward with his sword.

"What in heaven's name! You behold the three sixes on your left thigh; therefore, you carried the bastard twins. You shall die!"

A great number of people rushed out of their huts when they heard Rachel's cry, "Please have mercy on me; it was not I who planned such evil!"

King Victor gathered his men around the naked woman. As they started to remove their swords from their scabbards, a young priest from Rome appeared in the midst of the crowd.

"My dear Great King of Rome, it is written that the twins live; so must the woman!"

"Shut up, you Devil advocate," yelled King Victor. "These twins are the children of Satan. The whore shall die; so must the twins."

The priest handed over a scripture to one of the armor bearers, thinking it would persuade the King's mind. By this time, a prophet appeared just as the priest.

"This woman, Rachel, was once a virgin. Her virginity was taken from her by six men. One was Lucifer, the others his followers. It was not she who planned such evil to come into the world. It is written; it had to be done!"

Before the prophet could finish, King Victor furiously interrupted with a laugh, "You're no prophet. You slander the scripture."

"What scripture do you dictate these words from—The Book of Lies?"

"What I say is true," the Prophet spoke wildly. "If you kill the twins, they will resurrect, and one thousand years of living hell will come upon the earth."

"What year will these so-called twins resurrect?" asked King Victor.

"We shall not know the year, day or time, just as the coming of our Lord," answered the Prophet.

It was mentioned that King Victor raised his sword toward the Heavens, asking God for approval.

A strong wind blew from the north side, and the entire Earth shook! Tall buildings crumbled into pieces. People collapsed. Some village people believed it was the beginning of the end. What God echoed to King Victor that day was never mentioned.

It was later recorded that he commanded his men to kill the priest, Rachel, and even the Prophet.

The twins were cut out of Rachel's womb and then crucified on separate crosses.

King Victor believed that by burning the twins on crosses, they would never resurrect, and one thousand years of living hell on earth would never come to pass!

And if so, let this curse fall on future generations!

ABOUT THE AUTHOR

Mestat Imhotep is a Philadelphia native. He has been captivating readers with his bold and controversial horror stories since the ninth grade.

www.ingramcontent.com/pod-product-compliance
Lightning Source LLC
Chambersburg PA
CBHW060747180626
46818CB00002B/488